"What i[...] Dair asked

His voice now was soft with concern. "What's the matter?"

Jenna stared at him, seeing the moonlight glint in his eyes. For a moment, she was tempted to forget what she'd seen, to throw herself into his arms, lay her head on his shoulder and pretend that everything was as she'd always supposed it to be. That Dair loved her, after all, that they were embarking on the marriage she had dreamed of.

But even as her lips began to part for his kiss, she drew back. It wasn't that kind of a marriage, was it? It wasn't a marriage at all. And Dair knew that.

She could never forgive him.

"The matter?" she asked, her voice bitter. "Dair, you know what the matter is. We both know. Why pretend?"

Nicola West, born on the south coast of England, now lives in central England with her husband and family. She always knew she wanted to write. She started writing articles on many subjects, a regular column in a county magazine, children's stories and women's magazine stories before tackling her first book. Though she had three novels published before she became a Harlequin author, she feels her first novel for Harlequin was a turning point in her career. Her settings are usually places that she has seen for herself.

Books by Nicola West

HARLEQUIN ROMANCE

2526—DEVIL'S GOLD
2592—NO ROOM IN HIS LIFE
2610—WILDTRACK
2640—THE TYZAK INHERITANCE
2646—CARVER'S BRIDE
2669—TORMENTED RHAPSODY
2718—A ROOTED SORROW
2760—SKY HIGH
2771—COMEBACK
2884—HIDDEN DEPTHS
3089—SNOW DEMON
3101—A WOMAN'S PLACE

HARLEQUIN PRESENTS

589—LUCIFER'S BRAND
998—UNFINISHED BUSINESS

LAST GOODBYE
Nicola West

Harlequin Books

TORONTO • NEW YORK • LONDON
AMSTERDAM • PARIS • SYDNEY • HAMBURG
STOCKHOLM • ATHENS • TOKYO • MILAN

Original hardcover edition published in 1990
by Mills & Boon Limited

ISBN 0-373-03168-8

Harlequin Romance first edition December 1991

LAST GOODBYE

CHAPTER ONE

THE happiest day of her life.

That was what she had expected it to be. Wasn't it what they all said—that a girl's wedding day would be the happiest of her life? The day all her dreams came true in a haze of romance, a cloud of white lace, a drift of roses as red as the blood that dropped from a broken heart...?

Perhaps for most girls it was. Perhaps most girls did go into their new lives secure in the love of the man they had just married. Perhaps most girls didn't make a discovery on their wedding day that changed everything...

Jenna turned away from the bedroom door, her heart a searing pain that beat its way through her body, aching into the tips of her toes, into the throbbing fingertips that she held to her cold, white cheek. Her eyes were dry, burning with their need for tears she was too shocked to shed.

Perhaps later she would be able to find release in weeping—but there was no time now. People were waiting for her.

She must go into the other bedroom, the one her parents slept in, she must take off the floating dress of white chiffon and lace, lay it carefully on the wide bed and leave it for her mother to put away when they had gone. She must lift Aunt Mickie's pearl head-dress from her head and replace it in the box, brush out her honey-gold hair so that it fell loose and shining to her shoulders.

She must restore her make-up and dress herself in the skirt and jacket of soft green suede that made her eyes glow like the topaz earrings that she would fit into her ears in place of the pearl drops that had been Dair's first real gift to her. She must try not to remember the day he had given her the little box, the love that she had believed she saw in his eyes.

She must try to think of nothing but how to get through the next hour, until they had escaped their laughing guests and were alone at last.

And then...?

Jenna closed the bedroom door. In another moment, Dair would have glanced up and known that she had seen. And she wasn't ready yet for the truth she would read in his eyes.

Even though her heart was already crying it out, she wasn't prepared to see it in his face, to know that every moment leading up to this had been a lie. The revelation which had already begun would have to be resolved— but not yet. Not until they were alone, far from everyone they knew, with time for each other.

In a bitter daze, Jenna went through the motions of preparing to leave her wedding reception. Her mind seemed curiously detached, as if the real, essential part of her was standing back, watching, as her body performed its tasks.

She saw her wedding dress spread over the bed like a drift of foam and thought only briefly of the tremulous joy with which she had put it on only a few hours ago. She looked at the pearly head-dress and remembered how Dair's Aunt Mickie had placed it on her hair, whispering that she hoped it would bring her as much happiness as her own marriage had known.

And as she remembered, a cynical smile tugged momentarily at her lips. Happiness! What happiness could there be for her, knowing that her marriage was over before it had begun?

The suede jacket slipped easily over the cream silk shirt, and Jenna looked at herself in the mirror. Slender, of moderate height, with hair that swung like a bell just above her shoulders, dark brown eyes that were even larger than usual and a mouth that could widen into a happy smile that warmed every feature—but that was now straight, unsmiling, the soft lips trembling with pain.

That wouldn't do. She stretched it into a smile that was little more than a travesty, then summoned up all her determination and tried again and again until she looked more her normal self. Nobody waiting downstairs must know that anything had happened; nobody must see the tears that were in her heart, the pain that throbbed through every nerve.

Not even Dair.

Especially not Dair.

Jenna glanced at the thin gold wristwatch that had been his wedding present to her. There were still a few minutes before she need go down. A few minutes in which to pretend that everything was still all right.

That Dair really did love her, as she had believed he loved her all through their whirlwind courtship...

Jenna had met Dair Adams first in the office of one of her clients. She had been there for an hour or so, supervising the last-minute arrangements of the buffet, setting the food out in delicious array, arranging the flowers that set off the shining white linen, the sparkling silver and glass. Then, with everything ready and a quarter of an hour to go before her client brought the guests into the boardroom which was being used for the lunch, she had wandered to the wide windows and stood for a moment staring down at the bustle of the City of London.

Absorbed in watching the traffic and thinking wistfully of the quiet country village in which she had grown up, she hadn't heard the door open and close behind her. And when the newcomer spoke in her ear she was unable to prevent a jump of surprise.

'Sorry,' he said at once with smile. 'I didn't realise you hadn't heard me. It's this carpet—it's so thick an elephant could walk as softly as a cat. Usually I can be heard clumping about for miles around.'

Jenna recovered herself and looked at him. Tall, with dark hair and brilliant blue eyes, he looked as athletic as a panther and was probably just as soft-footed. She doubted very much whether he had ever 'clumped' in his life. She felt a sudden, unexpected kick of her heart.

'I didn't hear a thing—I was miles away,' she admitted, widening her mouth in the smile that was more attractive than she knew, lighting her cinnamon-brown eyes to sparkling topaz and bringing a luminous happiness to her mobile features. She saw his expression change, his eyes widen and then narrow, his dark brows quirking upwards at their outer corners, and then he returned her smile with a warmth that had been absent from his former air of remote politeness.

'Must have been a nice place to be,' he remarked, and Jenna nodded, still shaken by her reaction to this man.

'It is. I was thinking of my home—the village I come from in Warwickshire. So different from this.' She glanced down at the teeming streets. 'I can imagine just what it's like there at this moment. The trees and hedges will be coming into leaf, the lanes will be lined with primroses, the fields will be full of lambs frisking about...' She stopped and gave him an apologetic glance. 'Sorry—I'm making it sound like the picture on a chocolate box. And it's not—there's reality there too, birth and death and tragedy. In fact, it's all *more* real somehow. Down there——' she nodded at the unending traffic '—it's all rather unreal.'

'If you dislike London so much,' he said after a pause, 'why do you live here?'

'Oh, I don't really dislike it. There are a lot of things I enjoy—concerts, the theatres, museums, even the bustle sometimes. But sometimes—when the sun shines and makes the Thames glitter and people's window-boxes burst with colour—well, I just feel a bit homesick.' She turned and smiled at him again. 'It passes.'

'Does it?' His eyes moved over her, slowly, as if he were taking in every detail of her slender figure in a narrow cream linen skirt and plain black, softly draped silk top. 'Well, perhaps I——' He turned abruptly, a quick shadow of annoyance crossing his face as the boardroom door opened and a hubbub of voices preceded the chairman and his guests. 'Let's talk again later,' he muttered quickly. 'What's your name? I don't remember seeing you at the conference.'

'I'm Jenna Brooke. But——' Her words were lost in the chatter which had already swamped them, and before she could say any more several men had pushed themselves between her and the stranger, talking hard and gesticulating as they looked out of the window at the view that Jenna had been studying only moments before.

She looked round helplessly and caught the eye of the chairman, fixed on her in some surprise. Hastily, she remembered why she was here and made her way towards him.

'Everything's ready, Sir Leonard—if your guests would just like to help themselves. My girls are already serving the champagne—let me give you a glass.' She reached out for one of the trays being carried past and handed the glass to the large businessman who had hired her to cater for his lunch. 'I hope you'll find everything satisfactory,' she murmured, and smiled at him.

Sir Leonard Masham relaxed and nodded at her. He sipped his champagne and pursed his lips in appreciation. 'Certain I will, m'dear,' he said breezily. 'And I must say it's a nice touch, your circulating among my guests. Gives it a homely feeling. Always think a bit of feminine company does wonders for men after they've been talking business all morning—helps 'em wind down a bit, y'know.'

Jenna continued to smile, though she felt more like baring her teeth. She had already noticed that there were no women among Sir Leonard's guests, although she knew that there were women working successfully in his field. But to Sir Leonard, a businessman of the 'old school', successful before Women's Lib had begun to make any kind of mark, they were probably a joke, fluffy-headed secretary birds who were nothing more than a meaningless token to modern thinking.

He certainly wouldn't take them seriously. He wouldn't be taking Jenna herself seriously if she were not providing a successful buffet lunch for his guests. Doing a woman's work, in fact. She wondered if he expected her to sit down in a corner and produce some knitting.

But no. He'd be happy to have her mingling with his guests, looking decorative and adding the 'feminine touch'!

Huh! And no doubt all his guests, now gorging themselves on her delicious food, felt the same way. Including the tall, dark and definitely handsome stranger to whom she had found herself talking a few minutes before.

Jenna glanced round the long room and saw him talking with a group of other men. Taller than most of them, he looked relaxed and urbane in his dark suit, his expression serious yet with a flicker of humour never far away from his eyes. She watched him curiously; there was something about him that set him apart from the rest of the over-earnest businessmen who filled the room.

As she tried to define what it was, he glanced up and their eyes met. Jenna found herself staring into brilliant blue depths, unable to wrench her gaze away from his. Then the man next to him claimed his attention. He gave her one final, burning glance and turned away; and Jenna, suddenly aware that she had stopped breathing, took in a tiny gasp of air and turned blindly towards the door. Trembling a little, she escaped into the ante-room which was being used as a kitchen.

'Wow! What hit you?' asked Denise, her partner, pausing with a tray of *vol-au-vents*. 'You look as if you've seen the Ghost of Lunches Past.'

'Just do me a favour, Den, would you?' Jenna muttered, leaning against the wall. 'Find out who that tall man is—the one by the window.'

Denise peered through the door. 'The one with the film-star looks? Mm, definitely dishy. But I thought you didn't fancy business tycoons. Didn't you say they're all pompous yuppies with more money than sense and——?'

'Never mind what I said—just find out his name.' Jenna watched her friend sally out into the boardroom and closed the door behind her. 'I might just want to avoid him, mightn't I?' she muttered, and leaned her head against the door.

But she didn't want to avoid him. Even at that moment, she knew that. And by the time they were packing up, ready to leave the offices, Denise had found out his name and a good deal more about him.

'He's not a business tycoon at all!' she reported gleefully. 'He's a *farmer*, would you believe? Had a place in Suffolk, but he's sold up now and he's buying an estate down in Devon. That's why he's been at this lunch—Sir Leonard's got an estate there he wants to sell. And Dair Adams is thinking of buying it. So if you fancy a life among the cream and the pixies, Jenna——'

'Don't be a fool!' Jenna threw a tea-towel at her. 'I just wanted to know his name, that's all. Nothing more than that. I've certainly no interest in either cream or pixies, and I don't suppose I'll ever see Dair Adams again, so——'

But she was wrong. For at that very moment the door opened and Dair himself came in, as silently as he had approached Jenna across the thick carpet of the boardroom. With one swift glance, he took in the array of dirty dishes being piled up, ready to take back to Jenna's own kitchen for washing. He glanced briefly at Denise, standing with a tea-towel in her hand and her eyes and mouth wide open.

And then he looked at Jenna, trembling at the other side of the room.

'I said we'd talk again later,' he began abruptly. 'I've been looking for you everywhere.'

'Not quite everywhere,' Jenna said quickly. 'You didn't look here.'

'I didn't expect to find you here. I thought you were at the conference.' He cast a sweeping glance around at the debris of what had been a very good buffet. 'I didn't realise you were a—a——'

'Servant? Cook?' Jenna said sweetly. 'But if you knew Sir Leonard at all, you must have known he sees women only in those roles. This should have been the first place you looked—not the last.'

'I don't know him well. I'm just here to do business with him. And even if I had known——'

'Don't say you wouldn't have expected to find me doing such menial work,' Jenna advised him. 'I happen to be quite proud of what I do. And it's a job quite a few men do rather well, too.' Her brown eyes challenged him and Dair Adams stared at her for a moment, then ran his hand through hair that sprang like dark coils around his fingers.

'We seem to be getting off on the wrong foot—and I don't want that. I thought we were getting along rather well earlier on. Look, I'd like to talk to you. Can we meet—tomorrow evening, perhaps? Go to one of these concerts you enjoy, or a theatre?' His tone was oddly diffident, as if he were unused to asking for dates, but his eyes still had that strange, smouldering quality that hinted at something in him that both attracted and disturbed her. Something dangerous...something she knew instinctively could mean peril if she got involved with him. The kind of peril she didn't need...

'What do you say?' he asked again, and there was an appeal in his voice that she couldn't ignore.

She heard a muffled sound from Denise and made a mental note to throw more than a tea-towel at that young lady as soon as they were alone. If only Dair could have waited until her partner had taken a load of crockery to the car! Irritated, she was on the point of saying no—

and then she caught Dair's eye again and knew that she couldn't.

It wasn't just the appeal in his voice. Or the smouldering eyes. There was something else there. And in that moment, the room and all that was in it faded out of her consciousness. She looked into Dair's eyes and knew that she was in the grip of destiny, and powerless to fight it.

They met the next evening. Dair had tickets for a concert at the Festival Hall, but they never got there. Instead, he took her to a small French restaurant with checked tablecloths and a *patron* with a moustache and a white apron, who looked as if he ought to be back at home in Normandy running his own *auberge*.

They ate steaming bowls of *bouillabaisse* and cheeses from a huge board, accompanying both with crusty French bread such as Jenna had never seen outside Paris, and they drank French wine which surpassed any of those she normally served at her lunches. And they talked.

Or Jenna talked. Dair said little. He asked questions, and he watched her with those burning eyes as she answered. She told him about her home in Warwickshire—a small village near Stratford-upon-Avon, where her father worked as a civil servant and her mother was a receptionist with the local doctor. She told him about her two brothers, Stephen doing research in America, Scott at university, and she told him how and why she had come to London.

'I needed to break away a bit, so when I'd got my catering qualifications I found a job in one of the big hotels. I enjoyed it at first, but after a while I began to get restless—I wanted to work on my own. So Denise and I hit on this idea of doing catering for office functions. We'd done a few Christmas parties and we'd begun to get enquiries for lunches like the one you were at yesterday. It seemed as though there might be a market for it. We're both interested in the décor as well—the flowers and so on. I'd done floristry as my second subject and Denise is into interior decoration, so we make a good team. We think we offer something special, and we're kept busy enough to prove it.'

'You sound very proud of your business,' Dair commented.

'Yes, I am. We started with nothing but our skills and enough money to invest in basic kitchen equipment and some good plain crockery. Now we rent a proper kitchen and can afford to use good linen and glass as well as china. And we'll soon be taking on more staff—we already employ a woman to help prepare food and wash up, as well as the two waitresses, but we need another cook as well.'

'So you're expanding. And is that what you want?'

Jenna looked at him, startled. 'What we want? Well, of course it is. Doesn't everyone want to be a success?'

'Of course. But it depends what your definition of success is. For instance, do you really want to be head of a catering empire in London? Or do you really, deep down, want to go back to the country? To see the trees and hedges coming into leaf, the lanes lined with primroses, the lambs frisking about?' He kept his eyes on her face and she knew that he was taking note of her rising colour, the sudden tears in her eyes. 'I ask merely because you seemed rather lost yesterday,' he added gently after a few moments.

'You remembered everything I said,' Jenna managed to say past the ache in her throat, and he inclined his head. 'Why?'

He looked at her again, and this time his eyes were veiled, the smouldering emotion that she had sensed tightly contained. His voice was remote, even a little chilling.

'I don't know. That's what I need to find out.'

Jenna stared at him and was swept again, even more strongly, by the sense that this man spelt danger to her of a strange and ominous kind. Apprehension tingled over her skin and she knew that if she were wise she would make an end to this now. Tonight. Thank Dair Adams politely for a pleasant evening. Go straight home.

And never see him again.

The food in her mouth was suddenly tasteless. She laid down her knife.

'I—I think I ought to go now,' she said, and her voice shook.

Dair was on his feet at once.

'Of course. You must be tired. I imagine your work starts quite early in the morning—rather like mine.' She realised that he had said almost nothing about his own life, had encouraged her to talk about hers. 'Tomorrow evening?' he asked as the *patron* brought her jacket. 'We could try a concert again—we might even get there—or just eat, if that's what you'd prefer.' His eyes were on her again, insistent, compelling. She knew she must say no. To agree would be to invite...who knew what?

'I'll call for you at seven,' he said as his hired car drew up outside her block of flats, and Jenna nodded. And knew that somehow, at some deep unspoken level, she had committed herself.

From that night on, they were inseparable. Dair was in London for a week, during which time they saw each other every evening. They went to concerts and scarcely heard the music, theatres from which they came out with barely any idea about the play. They walked beside the Thames and saw the Houses of Parliament reflected in moon-bright water; they stood in Trafalgar Square and saw Nelson silhouetted against the stars while pigeons fluttered round his head looking for a roosting-place. They stared at the dark bowl of the sky, reluctant to let the night come to an end.

'I can't believe I haven't always known you,' Jenna said softly as they wandered slowly beside the Serpentine on an afternoon when daffodils danced and crocuses carpeted the grass with purple and gold. 'I can't remember what it was like not to have you in my life.'

Dair looked down at her, his face sombre. 'Can't you, Jenna?'

She frowned a little, troubled by his gaze. 'What is it, Dair?'

He shook his head. 'Nothing. Only... don't imagine there are no dark places in life, Jenna. None of us can ever know another person completely.' He paused, then added quietly, 'How much, for instance, do you know about me?'

'All I need to,' she answered lightly, but he shook his head again and she saw that he was serious. 'Well—I know that you were born in Suffolk and grew up on your father's farm, then went to Yorkshire to work with your grandfather for a while, then came back to Suffolk when your father died and farmed there. And now your grandfather's died too and left you his farm and you've decided to sell both and buy a large place in Devon. And——' she stopped and then finished lamely '—and that's about all.'

'Quite. No more, in fact, then any one of my acquaintances might know. Yet you feel you know all you need to know about me.'

'And so I do,' she insisted. 'I know what you're *like*— I know you're honest and honourable, if that doesn't sound too old-fashioned. I know you're kind and compassionate. I know you'd never do anyone a bad turn and I know you'd be absolutely loyal to anyone you considered a friend. And those things *are* all I need to know. Yes, I'd like to know your life-history too, but it comes second, don't you see?'

He stared at her, his dark brows drawn down over his eyes so that only a glimmer of blue showed between his lashes. Jenna had the feeling that something momentous was taking place behind those eyes. Something important to them both. She returned his look steadily, hiding the quivering in her heart.

'Yes, I see,' he said slowly. 'But I repeat what I say, Jenna. No one can know another person completely. There are always dark places... There's always a risk.'

'A risk we have to be prepared to take. Or there's no point in anything, is there?'

'No,' he said after another pause. 'No, I suppose there isn't.' He was silent for so long that she began to think he had forgotten her. And then, with a movement that was so abrupt that it made her jump, he turned and demanded, almost savagely, 'And are you prepared to take a risk, Jenna? With me? Are you prepared to take the biggest risk of all?'

His hands were gripping her arms so tightly that she almost cried out. She looked up into that tense face, the tormented blue eyes and knew that she must answer from her heart.

'What risk, Dair?' she asked huskily. 'What are you asking me?'

'To marry me, of course. What else?' His fingers were still tight on her arms, his eyes glittering with a passion she couldn't quite understand. It wasn't just the passion of a lover, which was only to be expected at such a moment—there was something else. Something deeper, stranger, as if some hidden compulsion were forcing him to take a course he had resolved always to avoid.

Almost as if his proposal came against his own will.

Once she had given Dair his answer, he seemed to relax, although Jenna had still at times been disconcertingly aware of that hidden torment that lay deep within him, too deep for her to probe. But there was too much to do, too many decisions to be made to allow much time for probing.

The business of changing over from one farm to another was complicated and time-consuming. Their marriage, they decided, would be best postponed until August, when everything should be settled and Dair would be firmly in control of the new farm on the edge of Dartmoor. Meanwhile, he took her several times to the family home in Suffolk, where his aunt still had a cottage which he was using as his base for the time being.

'You'll like Aunt Mickie,' he said as they travelled down for Jenna's first visit. 'She's been more like a mother to me since Mum died when I was twelve. Came in every day and made sure Dad and I didn't live in a pigsty, was always there when I came home from school—she could have moved in altogether when Uncle Hugh died, but she refused, said it was better for us to remain independent. *She* was the one who was independent—Dad and I'd have been lost without her.'

'She must miss you. Will she move down to Devon too?'

'Not Aunt Mickie! Now Dad's dead and I'm moving away, she's taking half the village under her wing. Not that a good many of them weren't already there—she'd never turn away anyone in trouble. I think there'd be a riot if she tried to leave now.'

Jenna imagined a plump, motherly woman with apple cheeks and a motherly bosom. She was slightly disconcerted by her first glimpse of Aunt Mickie. Surely this thin scrap of woman couldn't be Dair's second mother, the woman half a village turned to in times of trouble? Then she noticed the bright blue eyes with their spark of humour, the energy in the fingers that were run frequently through springing grey curls, and revised her opinion.

And Aunt Mickie's first words confirmed her impression of a wire so live it quivered with its own self-engendered electricity.

'So you're Jenna!' They were ushered up the path of the cottage garden from the gate where they had been met. Jenna stood still for a moment under the bright regard. 'Yes. I can see what he means.' She didn't elaborate on this remark, but drew Jenna in through the low doorway. 'Tea's all ready for you, and then I've got to go out. Old lady down the road, dying. I promised to sit with her for an hour while her daughter gets out for some fresh air.' She glanced at Dair and added, 'Old Mrs Haggarty.'

'I'm sorry to hear that,' Dair said, gesturing to Jenna to sit down on a low, comfortably battered sofa beside a table almost buckling at the knees with sandwiches, scones and cakes. 'She's over ninety, isn't she?'

'Well over. I don't think she knows herself how old she is. Anyway, nothing to be sorry for. She's happy to go and it's peaceful enough, just fading away.' Aunt Mickie poured tea quickly and efficiently, pausing only to ask Jenna how she liked it. 'Not that many old people have the privilege of dying in their own homes any more.'

As tea progressed, she talked about the affairs of the village. Her voice was light and quick, like the twittering of a small bird, and her movements as swift, yet there was an air of restfulness about her that seemed to leave the air quiet where she had been.

Like a bird again, Jenna thought, bringing brightness with it on a gloomy day. She began to understand why so many people turned to Mickie Adams in times of need, and why Dair had looked on her as a second mother.

She'd had no children of her own, he had told Jenna. Instead, she had given her love generously to anyone who might need it—from himself, a motherless boy, to the oldest woman in the village. From stray cats, picked up and fed before being found good homes, to homeless tramps for whom she could not do as much—yet who came back time after time, knowing that at this cottage at least they would find a welcome. And never, in spite of all the warnings she had been given, taking advantage of her.

'Most of them do little jobs for her,' Dair had said as they drove down from London to this little corner of Suffolk. 'Clearing out drains, trimming hedges, that sort of thing. She keeps a shed cleared out for them to doss down in, with a few clean blankets... There aren't as many about now, of course. They're in the cities now, huddled in subways and Underground stations. I think she misses them, you know.'

Jenna had felt at home with Aunt Mickie almost at once. And they had spent many hours talking. But as the time for the wedding had drawn nearer, Jenna had found the older woman's eyes resting on her in a way that made her feel uncomfortable. As if there were something she hadn't been told; something she ought to know.

There was only a month to go before the wedding when she went down to Suffolk for a weekend without Dair, who was now busy with the estate in Devon.

'There wasn't really much point in my going this time,' she said as she sat with Aunt Mickie in the garden, watching the sunset. 'We've done as much as we can to the house and he's busy with the livestock and out-buildings—I'd hardly see him. And once we're married—well, Devon's an awful long way from Suffolk.'

'You think I'll be lonely?' Aunt Mickie asked with a humorous lift of her brows. 'With someone knocking on my door every half-hour? You don't need to worry about me, Jenna—not that I won't miss you both, of course.'

'I know. And I wasn't worrying about you, to be quite honest,' Jenna confessed. She looked at Mickie, started to say something, then stopped. Dair's aunt waited for a moment, then reached out and touched Jenna's arm.

'What is it, my dear? Are you worrying about the wedding? It's a big change for you, giving up your own business, your own life. Is that the problem? Are you afraid *you'll* be lonely?'

'Oh, no—no. As I told you, Denise has found a partner to buy out my share of the catering business and Dair's quite happy for me to start a business in Devon—probably in Tavistock, since that's the nearest town. I thought I might try floristry for a change... Anyway,

I'm sure I shan't be lonely. I'll have Dair, after all.' She was aware that her words sounded brave rather than convinced, but couldn't prevent the hint of anxiety that touched her voice. She still couldn't quite believe what had happened to her—the instant chemistry, almost a conflagration, that had crackled between herself and Dair from that first meeting; the fact that she was prepared to jettison everything she'd worked for to be his wife. Yet it was the plain and simple truth. Dair had become the most important factor in her life.

'Then what are you afraid of? That Dair doesn't love you after all?' There was just enough humour in her tone to allow Jenna to treat the question as a joke if she wanted to, and enough gravity to encourage her to confide in the older woman. She hesitated for a moment, then made up her mind.

'I'm sure he loves me, Aunt Mickie. I don't believe he'd marry me if he were in any doubt. You see, one of the things I admired most about Dair from the very beginning was his honesty. His total integrity. I don't believe he'd ever deceive me in that way.'

'But he might deceive himself?'

Jenna considered, then shook her head.

'I don't think so.' But her tone was not quite so certain and Mickie regarded her thoughtfully.

'How much has Dair told you about himself, Jenna?'

Jenna turned her head. Their eyes met.

'He's told me about Lysette, if that's what you mean,' Jenna said quietly, and saw Dair's aunt relax slightly. 'He hasn't made any secret of the fact that he was engaged before, Aunt Mickie.'

She closed her eyes for a moment, remembering the night he had told her, the difficulty he had had in recounting the brief story. It was almost as if he was ashamed of having been in love before—yet he was almost thirty-six; it would have been surprising if he had not.

She'd told him this, adding with a teasing smile that she wouldn't ask questions about his harem if he didn't ask about her string of lovers. But it had been the wrong thing to say; for once Dair's sense of humour seemed to have deserted him and it had taken her the rest of the evening to coax him out of his sombre mood.

'Has he told you *all* about Lysette?' Mickie asked. 'How it—finished?'

Jenna shook her head. 'He obviously didn't want to talk about it, Aunt Mickie. I just know that they met when her father bought Prior's Redding, about fifteen miles from here. I imagine she was rather beautiful——' unconsciously she ran a hand through her own gleaming hair '—and Dair fell quite hard. It lasted two or three months and then—well, just fell apart, I suppose. Anyway, it was three or four years ago now and as he said, it's all in the past and has nothing to do with us.'

'And he didn't want to talk about it,' Mickie said softly.

'No.' Jenna discovered with irritation that her voice was a shade higher than usual. 'So I didn't press him. He's right—it's in the past.'

Mickie was silent for a moment. Then she said, 'Jenna, my dear, nothing that happens to us is ever truly in the past. It's with us, a part of us, for the rest of our lives. Dair doesn't want to tell you everything that happened between him and Lysette. I think he should. I think one day he *must*—and you must let him. But until then—let him keep his silence.'

'You mean I shouldn't ask him,' Jenna said, looking at the sunset.

'No. Don't ask him.' Mickie turned her head towards Jenna and Jenna, sensing the movement, met her eyes. They looked at each other for a long moment, then Mickie repeated with quiet intensity, 'Don't ever ask him, Jenna. Don't ever ask him about Lysette.'

It hadn't been too difficult. There had been too much to do during the following month to let a half-forgotten romance occupy her mind. Immediately after that weekend, she had gone back to London to finalise her agreement with Denise and hand the business over to her. Then she had gone to Warwickshire, to stay with her parents and pack up the few belongings that were still at home while she prepared for her wedding in the little village church where she had been baptised.

Her wedding day had come in a haze of morning mist, clearing away to reveal a day of golden August sunshine, and it seemed that the whole village was there to see her married.

Jenna had not believed that so much happiness was possible. She came to the church door with Dair, her fingers on his arm, the warmth of his body close beside her. She looked up into his face and saw his eyes, clear and blue and dark with love, looking deep into her heart, and if anyone had told her then that he carried the memory of another woman in his heart she would have laughed them to scorn.

All through the reception—through the line of guests wishing her happiness, through the wedding breakfast, through the speeches and the cutting of the cake and the champagne and toasts—she drifted on her cloud of happiness. And so it was all the more painful when she looked through the bedroom door and realised with a shock how flimsy the foundations of her happiness had been.

It was time to go down. Jenna took a deep breath and tugged her jacket into place. *Nobody* must know.

Once again she remembered the little scene that had been branded on her eyes. Dair, almost ready to go on honeymoon with her, taking a photograph from his case and staring at it. A photograph, as she could see from the door, of a beautiful woman, a woman with long, ash-blonde hair and slanting green eyes. An unforgettable face, and one he stared at with deep and bitter regret.

She remembered his voice as he touched the picture to his lips.

'I'm sorry, Lysette. So sorry...'

CHAPTER TWO

LYSETTE. Lysette. Lysette.

The name hammered through Jenna's brain all the way to the airport. Dair, driving, was also silent. She was aware that he glanced at her once or twice but she didn't turn her head. It wasn't time yet to meet those dark blue eyes, to know that they were, after all, lying to her. That she'd tied herself to a man who didn't love her after all, who was still in love with another woman...

Why? *Why?*

The question alternated with the name in her mind, creating a cruel, tormenting rhythm. Why should Dair want to marry her if he was still in love with Lysette? Why had he and Lysette parted? Why?

Aunt Mickie had known. She'd been aware from the beginning that there was something wrong. She'd hinted as much, that evening in the garden when they'd talked. Why hadn't she told Jenna what she knew then?

Why had she warned Jenna never to ask about Lysette?

And what was she to do now? Would Dair continue with this pretence—look at her with the vivid eyes she had trusted so implicitly, touch her with the fingers that had been so gentle, so tender? Make love to her...?

Oh, lord. Make love to her. The moment they'd waited for—*she'd* waited for—with such passionate yearning. The moment that would now be as empty as a cracked bucket.

How could she let him make love to her?

The airport was only a short drive from Jenna's parents' house. They were followed part of the way by cheering guests, led—naturally—by Jenna's brothers Stephen and Scott, together with Rob Preston, who had lived next door ever since they were all children and was now teaching at the local comprehensive school. Not very happily, Jenna had guessed when they talked at the reception, but there hadn't been time to go into it then. Anyway, he seemed lively enough as he kept his battered red Mini close behind them, hooting whenever he thought their attention might have wandered. Dair glanced into the mirror impatiently.

'D'you think they're intending to come all the way?'

'Not all the way to France, no. Just the airport.' She was surprised to find her voice sounding fairly normal, no more than a little tight. Dair shifted his glance sideways.

'Are you all right, Jenna?'

'Of course.'

'You seem rather quiet.'

'Just tired. It's been—quite a day.' And not the sort of day she'd expected, either. She closed her eyes and felt him touch her knee briefly.

'Never mind.' His voice sounded as tender as ever, and the tears stung her eyelids. For a moment, she wished she'd never seen him with Lysette's photograph, never known the truth. 'In a couple of hours we'll be in France, and we can relax.'

Relax. She didn't think she would ever relax again. She heard the hooting from behind and mentally consigned her brothers and Rob to outer darkness. If only they hadn't decided to carry on the fun and follow her and Dair to the airport. Now she was going to have to keep that bright, artificial smile pinned to her face and maintain the fiction of being a happy bride for even longer. When all she really wanted to do was to find some quiet little corner somewhere and die...

But it couldn't last forever. Nothing lasted forever. In a few hours, as Dair said, they would be alone. And then... She shook her head. She couldn't even begin to imagine it.

The *auberge* was small, an old inn standing back from a narrow country road in its own garden. Behind it ran a wide, shallow stream, its clear waters allowing the sun to light up the smooth blue pebbles. A few small fish darted about in a shoal, like children playing, and in the shadow of a willow a larger fish hung almost motionless, only its tail wafting slowly to and fro, like a guardian.

Jenna stood quite still on the grassy bank. Dair had chosen an idyllic honeymoon spot. He must have known it before. Had he been here with Lysette?

She sat down on the grass and leaned against the willow, closing her eyes. Her thoughts had given her no respite. On the plane, she had pretended to be asleep, her hand clasped loosely in Dair's. The warmth and strength of his fingers had brought fresh pain to her heart.

She wanted nothing more than to open her eyes and look into a face filled with love—but she knew that the love must be false, the eyes untrue, the mouth telling lies and she couldn't bear it.

Oh, Dair, why? her heart cried. Why did you do this to me? Why tell me you love me, why *marry* me, when all the time you're still in love with her?

Getting through Customs and picking up their hire car had created a welcome bustle, and for a while she'd been able to behave as if there was nothing wrong. And during the short drive from the airport to the quiet village where they were to spend their brief honeymoon Dair had chatted easily, and she'd had to do no more than make the occasional response.

Now they were here and, while Dair was talking to the *patron*, Jenna had taken the opportunity to slip out into the garden. And she knew that the moment of truth was drawing near. Soon, Dair would come out into the garden to find her. He would drop down to the grass beside her and gaze into the clear running water, his cheek against hers, his fingers stroking her skin.

And then he would suggest that they go and get ready for dinner—go to that low-ceilinged room under the eaves, with the big double bed which they would have to share that night...

I can't, she thought agonisedly. I can't.

She threw a quick glance back at the low building. It was like a cat, asleep in the warmth of the sun. Dair and the *patron* could be seen just inside the doorway. In another moment he would be outside, walking across the lawn towards her.

Jenna jumped to her feet and walked swiftly to the edge of the lawn, where a small wood marked the boundary of the garden. A narrow, twisting path led through them, and she followed it, curbing the desire to break into a run. It was crazy, she knew—she was going to have to face Dair some time. But not now, she prayed, stumbling over roots and trailing briars, not for a little while. Give me time—I must have time.

Behind her, she could hear footsteps. He must have seen her leave the garden; he was following her through the wood.

Jenna felt a bubble of panic rising in her throat. She quickened her step.

'Jenna! Jenna, wait for me.'

A tiny sob choked her. She was half running, her hands stretched out in front of her to ward off the branches that hung low over the path.

'Jenna, what are you doing? *Wait* for me—you'll hurt yourself. Jenna—darling—what's the matter?'

He was close to her now. Her reason gone completely, Jenna gave a little cry of fear. She turned her head towards him and tripped over a log, half hidden in last year's fallen leaves. She hit the ground with a thump and lay winded for a moment, staring up with frightened eyes.

Dair knelt beside her, his face concerned. He touched her cheek with gentle fingers. She could have sworn that the love in his eyes was real.

'Darling, whatever did you do that for?' he asked. 'Running away like that...what got into you? It was almost as if you were frightened.'

Frightened? Had she really been frightened? As she lay there, Jenna thought back over the last few minutes and knew that she had been afraid—but of what? Not Dair, surely.

Even if he had lied to her, pretended to love her, married her for reasons she couldn't begin to comprehend—even then, did she need to fear him? Or was it fear of a confrontation with him that had driven her to run like that? Fear of knowing the truth?

And then she remembered the sensation she'd had when they first met. That Dair Adams spelled danger. That, if she got involved with him, she would be asking for trouble.

As the thoughts chased themselves through her mind, she saw Dair's face change, saw the concern in his eyes darken and turn to something else. Bewilderment...suspicion? She didn't know. Perhaps, she thought with a lurch of her heart, she didn't know very much about Dair at all...

'What's the matter, Jenna?' he asked quietly.

Jenna shook her head and turned her face away, pressing her cheek against the cool earth.

'Jenna!' His hands were on her shoulders, pulling her up against him. She felt the warmth of his body through the thin shirt he wore, felt the pounding of his heart against her breast. 'Jenna, my love,' he murmured, and his lips were on her face, her neck, her ears. One hand caught at the nape of her neck, holding her head up as his mouth roamed across her scorched skin. His fingers strayed to her breast and trembled across the soft roundness, then pulled gently at the buttons on her blouse.

As she felt the thin fabric part, a cool breeze touching skin that was barely covered by the lace of her bra, Jenna twisted in Dair's arms, pulling herself roughly away from him. She heard his gasp of surprise and felt her own pang that this wasn't for real, that it was only a sham. And then she was a yard away, crouching on the forest floor staring at him like an animal at bay.

'Jenna!'

Surely that was honest bewilderment she saw in his eyes? For a split second, Jenna felt a surge of hope— couldn't she have been mistaken after all?

But common sense trampled hard on her wistful hopes. Of course he was surprised; yes, and bewildered too. He didn't know she'd seen him with that photograph of Lysette. As far as he was concerned, nothing had changed. Jenna was as much in love with him as ever, and must believe that he loved her too.

The trouble was, she *was* still in love with him—or wanted to be. And that made her position all the more perilous.

There was nothing more dangerous to a woman than being in love with a man who was only using her. Unless it was being married to him.

She got up slowly, keeping her eyes fixed on his face as he rose too. But when he tried to come near her again she shook her head and raised a palm as if warding him off.

What was he using her *for*? Why, why had he married her?

'Jenna, what is it? What's the matter? You're acting like a frightened schoolgirl. You're not scared of me, surely?' His vivid blue eyes searched her face. 'I can't believe it,' he said slowly. 'You can't be afraid of me. I'm your husband.'

Jenna swallowed. She knew that what she said and did now was crucial to her future. Whatever Dair's reasons for doing what he'd done, he was expecting her to play the faithful and loving wife. Half of her still longed passionately to do just that. The other half said no. *No.*

'Being my husband doesn't give you the right to—to assault me in a wood,' she said in a shaking voice.

Dair's brows came together in a hard, black line.

'*Assault* you? What in hell's name do you mean by that, Jenna? I just wanted to kiss you, that's all. Hell, we're married, aren't we? We're on our *honeymoon*. What do you expect, for heaven's sake?'

Jenna shook her head, closing her eyes against the tears she felt threatening to fall.

'I know we're married. I could hardly have failed to notice that.' That was better. Maybe sarcasm would come to her aid. 'It doesn't mean to say you can throw me down on the ground and jump on me the minute we arrive,' she went on haughtily. 'We do have a bedroom to go to, I understand.'

'So that's it. Well, I'd never have suspected you of being too prim to make love under the sky.' Dair looked at her, still frowning, obviously still hurt by her rejection. 'Is that really all it is, Jenna?'

Now was the moment she ought to tell him. But how could she say, baldly, that she'd seen him kissing the photograph of another woman? She hesitated, knowing that she should. The question of Lysette should be resolved between them before it became an issue too great to surmount.

But wasn't it that already? Hadn't Dair started this long ago by evading the issue of his previous engagement? Hadn't Aunt Mickie aided and abetted him by warning Jenna never to ask questions?

Hadn't it always been impossible for her to ask?

Impatiently, Jenna flicked back her hair and took a step forward. But before she could open her mouth, Dair's expression changed again and he laid his hands on her shoulders and smiled down at her.

'I'm being a fool, aren't I?' he said softly. 'A stupid, crass fool. Of course it'll be more romantic in that bedroom with its big soft bed and its low ceiling and beams. And the scent of honeysuckle coming in the window.' He turned and tucked her hand under his arm. 'I'm sorry, Jenna. I got carried away, I'm afraid. Put it down to the fact that I love you so much. And let's go back, before it happens again!'

He led her swiftly back through the woods, his arm firmly imprisoning her fingers, and the moment had passed. Once again, Jenna was assailed by doubts. It was almost impossible to look into those dark blue eyes and not believe them, to listen to his warm, deep voice and think that it was telling lies. She wanted so desperately to believe that Dair loved her.

But the picture of him standing in that bedroom, with Lysette's photograph in his hands, looking down at it with such longing, such regret, could not be wiped from her mind. It had happened. She had seen it. It could not be denied.

And the problem of what she was going to do about it was no nearer being solved than it had been then.

As slowly as if she were climbing a scaffold, Jenna mounted the narrow, crooked stairs to the bedroom.

Dair had gone out for a final walk down to the stream—the tactful, traditional behaviour of a bride-groom on his wedding night, leaving the bride to array herself in seductive lace and silk for their first encounter.

It had seemed so romantic when she'd thought about it before today, when she'd chosen her own nightgown, a dream of floating chiffon and satin ribbons. Now, it all seemed empty and hollow.

She opened the door and went into the room, crossing to the window to stare down at Dair's figure, dark and slender in the moonlight.

What would most young women think of her now? she thought ironically. From the very beginning, she and Dair had agreed that theirs should be an old-fashioned courtship, with all the romance of holding hands, exchanging kisses that only gradually deepened into passion, with the full declaration of their love kept for their wedding night. The yearning that had grown between them as the date grew nearer added to the sweetness of their romance, they had agreed. And they had looked forward all the more to the night when it would be all over and all restrictions cast aside.

'We'll have all our lives to make love to each other,' Dair had said, his eyes as dark as a midnight sea as he held her against him. 'But we'll never have this time again.' And she had agreed, feeling a faint pity for all those girls who went to bed with a man on the first— and sometimes only—date and never knew what a real, old-fashioned romance could be like.

Now she wondered a little bitterly if she had been a fool. Was there some other, darker reason why Dair had refrained from making love to her before they were married? Some reason that also had something to do with the breaking up of his engagement to Lysette...?

Jenna shivered and turned away from the window. But she did not start to undress. Instead, she sat down in a chair and tried to control her galloping thoughts.

It was stupid to let her imagination run away with her. But supposing there was something...something that Lysette had discovered about him, something that had killed her love for him? Something he couldn't risk Jenna's discovering too...until she was safely married to him?

You're being ridiculous, she told herself angrily. Turning this whole thing into some crazy mystery. You've been reading too many thrillers.

But what other reason could there be for Dair's having married her when he was so clearly still in love with another girl...?

She looked down into the garden again. It was still and quiet. Dair's silhouette had disappeared. Blended with the shadows? Or on his way back to the inn— through the door—coming up the stairs?

Jenna felt her heart lurch and then begin to thump raggedly. She looked towards the door, waiting for it to open. In a few moments he would be here.

She closed her eyes. It had been clear, during their meal, that Dair realised there was something wrong. Without the demands of the journey to divert his attention, she'd been unable to hide her discomfort when he touched her hand or her lack of response when he smiled into her eyes.

He'd said nothing; merely frowned a little and then lapsed into silence. Perhaps, she thought hopefully, he had simply assumed that she was tired after the bustle of the day. If she could just stave off any questions until tomorrow...

And just what good would that do? Dair wasn't going to be held at arm's length indefinitely. She knew him well enough now to know what that particular set to his firm lips meant. He might have decided not to question her any further during dinner—but he intended to find out just what lay behind her sudden change in attitude towards him, and before very many more hours had passed, too.

Well? She intended to tell him... didn't she?

With a sudden miserable ache in her throat, Jenna faced the fact that telling Dair what she had seen, what she now knew, was going to be just about the most difficult task she had ever undertaken. Because she didn't want to hear him admit that it was true. She didn't want to look into his eyes and know without any shadow of doubt that he loved another woman; that their marriage was, for whatever reason, a sham.

The door opened and, even though she'd been expecting it, Jenna gave a little jump. One hand halfway to her throat, she stared with wide eyes across the moonlit room.

'Not in bed yet?' Dair said quietly. He stood just inside the room, dark against the light from the passage, and then softly closed the door. 'I expected to find you ready for me . . . eager, even.'

There was a note in his voice she'd never heard before. A note of bitter irony. Jenna felt the colour scorch into her cheeks and was thankful that the room was too dim for Dair to see it. She swallowed, watching him cross the room towards her. She felt transfixed, as though his very presence paralysed her.

'What is it, Jenna?' he asked, and the irony had left his voice now, leaving it soft with concern. He crouched down in front of her, taking her hands in his. 'What's the matter?'

Jenna stared at him, seeing the moonlight glint in his eyes. For a brief moment she was tempted to forget what she had seen, to throw herself into his arms, lay her head on his shoulder and pretend that everything was as she had always supposed it to be. That Dair loved her after all, that they were embarking on the marriage she had dreamed of, the kind of marriage that normally happened only in romantic novels.

But, even as her lips began to part for his kiss, she drew back. It wasn't that kind of marriage, was it? It wasn't even the kind of marriage that most people ended up with—with high spots and low spots, long humdrum patches and a slow, gradual process of growing together.

It wasn't a marriage at all. And Dair knew that.

She could never forgive him.

'The matter?' she asked, and she could hear the bitterness in her own voice. 'Dair, you know what the matter is. We both know. Why pretend?'

For a moment, he was absolutely still. She felt his fingers grow rigid around hers, then tighten cruelly. A tingle of fear prickled across her skin. What did she know of this man, after all? She'd thought she knew everything she needed to—yet, in the most fundamental thing of all, she had been mistaken. What other mistakes might she have made?

'Dair——' she began, but his voice cut across hers, hard and cold as ice.

'You're going to have to explain that statement, Jenna. And fast.'

Her nerves flared.

'Am I? And do you think *you* have nothing to explain, Dair?'

He stared at her. 'I? No, I don't—nothing that I didn't need to explain yesterday, when you seemed happy enough to marry me. Nothing's changed since then, Jenna. Why in hell's name are you behaving like this? What do you think has happened?'

Jenna looked at him, searching his face for the truth. But she could no longer read his expression. It was as if he had closed himself away from her. Or perhaps she never had been able to read him? Perhaps it had all been an illusion?

'Has anyone been talking to you?' he asked suddenly.

'Talking to me? About what? What do you think they might have been saying?'

'Well, *I* don't know, do I?' he expostulated. 'I'm just trying to find out what's behind this—this change in attitude. Jenna, last night I could have sworn you loved me as much as I loved you—that you wanted me as much as I wanted you. Lord, it was so hard to leave you... And now you look at me as if you'd never seen me before. Why? *Why?* What *happened?*'

'You really don't know?' she said dully, and he shook his head.

'I don't. I swear I don't.'

'And you swear you love me? That you've married me because of love—for no other reason?'

'What is this? Didn't you hear the vows I made? Didn't I say just that?' He gripped her shoulders and shook her. 'What else do I have to do to convince you, for heaven's sake?'

Jenna looked into his eyes, holding his gaze steadily. It had to be said. The question had to be asked. And once again, in her mind, she heard Aunt Mickie's voice warning her never to ask it...

'Tell me about Lysette,' she said quietly. And felt his withdrawal.

Dair stood up. He stared out of the window for a long moment. Then he looked down at Jenna.

'Lysette has nothing to do with us,' he said. 'You have to believe that, Jenna.'

But there was a strange note in his voice. A tremor, a faint harshness as if some powerful emotion threatened to overwhelm him. And Jenna saw again the picture that had barely left her mind ever since she had stood at the bedroom door and watched him with the photograph. She saw him lift the picture, touch it with his lips. She looked up at him and shook her head. 'I can't.'

His shrug was so faint it was barely noticeable. And then he turned away. 'In that case,' he said quietly, 'there's nothing more to be said. You'd better get ready for bed, Jenna. It's all right,' he added as she hesitated, 'I won't make any...unwelcome demands.'

At the bitterness in his voice, Jenna felt the colour scorch over her whole body. The heat of tears in her eyes, she watched as he stepped out of the moonlight and went into the bathroom. The light snapped on and the door closed behind him.

As hastily as if she were afraid of being caught in some nefarious deed, Jenna scrambled out of her clothes. She hesitated over the frothy nightdress, then crammed it back into her suitcase. A long white silk shirt, intended for wearing with trousers, lay on a chair and she pulled it around herself and fastened the buttons with shaking fingers. Then she slipped into the wide bed and lay wide-eyed on the edge.

She was still awake when Dair came softly out of the bathroom. She heard him undress in the dark, then felt him lift the bedclothes and slide in beside her. Rigid, she waited. But the touch she half feared, half longed for, never came. Instead, after a few moments, she heard the soft, regular sound of breathing and knew that he was asleep.

Asleep! So that was all it meant to him.

And it was that, more than anything that had gone before, which convinced Jenna that she was right.

Their marriage was nothing but a sham.

CHAPTER THREE

THE leaves of the horse-chestnut trees were tinged with bronze when Jenna left the farmhouse and walked across the flagged yard to the garage where her car was kept. She paused for a moment, looking up past the big grey house to the moors, where the bracken was tawny with autumn colour. A few Dartmoor ponies were grazing there and some of Dair's sheep moved slowly across the short turf. High up in the clear blue sky she could see a buzzard circling slowly.

The beauty caught at her heart and she trembled with sudden yearning. If only the house were a real home. If only it contained love...

In the six weeks since she and Dair had been married, Jenna was still no closer to an answer to her questions about Lysette. She had tried again on the morning after their wedding, when she had woken to find herself lying close against Dair's body and discovered that he was naked.

In those first moments, she had been shaken by a desire that was almost too strong to be resisted. Oh, Dair, Dair, she had thought, remembering the times when they had held each other close and kissed with all the passion and longing known to lovers down the ages. How different she had expected this morning to be, waking for the first time in his arms after a night of discovery and delight. And she wished passionately that they had not waited for their marriage to complete their love. At least she would have had the memory of delight to hold now.

But that would only have made it worse, she realised at once. It would have made the knowledge of his betrayal all the more painful.

She turned her head to look at Dair. He was lying half turned towards her, dark hair tousled above a face that looked peaceful in sleep, the frown she had seen there last night smoothed out, leaving him looking younger, more vulnerable. Her heart ached as she watched him. It was almost impossible to believe that he could marry her while still loving another woman. And she was no nearer to understanding his reasons.

Jenna was shaken by a sudden longing to forget, to pretend—if only for a moment—that all was as it should be between them. She lifted her hand, began to trace his features with one finger moving gently just above his skin. Her hand trembled a little over his lips. And at that moment, Dair woke. He opened his eyes and looked straight into hers. His lips moved, and brushed against her hand.

'Jenna...' he murmured, and shifted in the bed, coming close against her. She felt the warmth of his skin tingle through the thin fabric of the shirt she wore, and gasped. Her heart thudded and she looked at him, her eyes wide and dark, her lips parted.

'*Jenna!*' His arms were round her, drawing her hard against him, and with one hand in the hair that lay like a flame across the pillow, he pulled back her head for his kiss. Jenna felt his lips take hers, soft but firm, opening her mouth against his and stilling her protest, reshaping it to a response that she could not deny.

She closed her eyes, summoning up all her will-power to fight the invasion of her senses. She must not give in to this hunger that raged through her, this clamour for his skin against hers, his lips on her mouth, her throat, her breasts...not even once must she allow herself to experience the soaring pleasures that she knew instinctively she could find so easily with Dair.

His hand was on her breast, warm and sensuous, his body stretched against hers. She could feel her muscles softening, her bones melting. In another second she would be past resistance...in another second it would be too late...in less than a second... With a swift, frantic movement she twisted away from him, wrenching her mouth away from his with a force that tore at her heart, turning her head, pushing with the hands that had so nearly tightened around his shoulders to hold him close.

'Jenna, what...?' He reached for her again and Jenna kicked herself away from him, her bare toes catching him painfully on the shin. She heard his muttered exclamation, then felt herself tip over the edge of the bed. Scrabbling wildly at the sheets, she slid to the floor, landing with a thump amid a flurry of bedclothes, with her pillow over her face. She lay helplessly entangled.

Dair knelt above her. He pulled away the pillow and Jenna looked up into his face.

'Please,' she whispered, 'please, Dair, don't touch me again.'

His eyes were dark, his mouth a hard line. He shook his head slowly and Jenna felt a tremor of fear. She pulled the bedclothes around her body and sat up, shifting away from him as she did so, humiliatingly aware of the picture she must present.

'Let me get this straight,' Dair said quietly. 'I'm not to touch you at all, right? Not kiss you, not hold you, not make love to you. That's what you want, that's what you're saying?'

No, it's not what I want at all, Jenna wanted to cry out. I *want* you to hold me, kiss me—I *want* you to make love to me. But only if you love me. And we both know that you don't.

Aloud, her voice shaking, she said, 'Yes. That's what I want.'

Dair stared at her. Then he slid over to the other side of the bed. He stood for a moment, his slender yet well-muscled body taut and hard, then reached for a dressing-gown and wrapped it around himself. He came over to Jenna and dropped her own silky négligé over her. Then he sat down again on the side of the bed.

'You'd better get up.' He waited until she had extricated herself from the sheets and wrapped her trembling body in the négligé. 'It's all right, Jenna,' he said curtly as she hesitated. 'You needn't look so scared. I'm not going to have my wicked way with you—not now, at any rate.' His tone turned the words into a threat, and she shivered, knowing that if Dair took her now it would be in no mood of delightful discovery, but rather as a punishment. Cautiously, she sat down in the basket chair by the window and looked at him.

'Dair——' she began, but he cut her short.

'Put me right if I've got this wrong. Did we, or did we not, get married yesterday?'

Jenna nodded.

'So we're on our honeymoon now? I'm not mistaken about that?'

Again she nodded. She watched him run his fingers through tousled black hair.

'So what in hell's name has got into you, Jenna? Why don't you want us to make love? You wanted it before, I'll swear you did. Or are you just a very good actress? Was it all a sham—did you never love me at all?' He stared at her, his eyes narrowing. 'Is that the truth,

Jenna? Did you have some other reason for marrying me? Tell me!'

Jenna gazed at him. She shook her head wordlessly. The temptation to let him think just that was almost too great to withstand. Wouldn't it be easier, after all, if he did? Couldn't they simply leave it at that—admit they'd made a mistake and part before any more damage was done?

But she couldn't do it. All her instincts cried out against it. She could not face Dair and tell him that the vows made yesterday had been entirely cynical—even though she believed that, for his part, that was just what they had been.

'Just leave it, Dair,' she muttered at last. 'Just let it go, will you? There's nothing else we can say.'

'*Nothing?*' The word exploded from him, and Jenna shrank back. 'How can there be nothing? We haven't even begun yet. No!' With a single movement he was on his feet and standing over her, his hands on her shoulders, shaking her with a violence that brought terror leaping into her throat. 'There's everything to say, Jenna. Everything! You've got to tell me what this is all about— why you've suddenly turned away from me. I've got to know, don't you understand that?' His eyes blazed down into hers and she could have sworn there was real torment in them. 'Jenna, for goodness' sake——'

'Let me go!' Her anger was rising now to match his. 'Let go, Dair! Take your hands away—you're hurting me.' He looked down at his fingers, biting into her shoulders, as if he had not known what he was doing. He removed them slowly, and Jenna rubbed the burning skin. 'All right, so you want to talk,' she spat at him. 'So *tell me about Lysette*.'

At once, his face changed. Anger and pain chased each other across his features, to be followed by a set obstinacy. When he looked down at her again, his eyes were veiled.

'I've already told you, Jenna,' he said, and his words were like stones dropped one by one into a bottomless well, 'Lysette has nothing to do with you and me. It's over, that part of my life—completely over.'

'I only wish I could believe you,' she answered quietly, and watched him turn away.

After that, it was obvious to them both that there was no point in continuing with a honeymoon. In silence, they dressed and went down to breakfast. The smiles of the *patron* and his wife faded before their sober faces and their croissants and coffee were brought quickly. They looked sorry, but not surprised, when Dair told them that he and his wife would be leaving at once.

'No sense in continuing with the charade,' he said grimly as he threw into his case the few items he had unpacked the day before. 'We'd better call it a day and go straight home.' His mouth twisted a little at the word. 'I don't imagine we'll have any difficulty in getting a flight.'

Jenna said nothing. Her heart ached as if it had been physically bruised. Her throat felt swollen, her eyes heavy. Silently, she gathered together her toilet things and the white shirt she had worn in bed, now crumpled and creased. She looked around the bedroom. The sheets were tumbled, the pillows out of shape, but the loving she had imagined had never taken place. The room was sterile, like the marriage which had promised so much.

'I expect you'd like me to remove the things I've taken down to Devon,' she said at last. 'Do you mind if I send for them? I don't think I can face going there mys——'

Dair whipped round. 'Remove them? What are you talking about, Jenna? What do you mean?'

'What I say, of course. You won't want me there any more than I want to come. I'll go back to London—I can cancel the sale of my flat. I know Denise has a new partner now, but——'

Dair crossed the room swiftly and took her by the shoulders, his hands hard on flesh already bruised by his earlier shaking.

'Stop taking nonsense, Jenna. You're not going anywhere. You're coming to Devon with me, do you hear? You're my wife—at least, as far as everyone else is concerned—and you're going to stay that way. Is that understood?'

'But——'

'I'm not having this marriage break down,' he said with grim finality. 'If you want to leave me, Jenna, you're going to have to find some very good reason. And make it public.' His eyes bored into hers. 'And simply refusing to make love with me on our wedding night isn't going to carry a lot of weight.'

Jenna stared at him. She swallowed, then said in a small voice, 'What are you saying, Dair?'

'I'm saying that if you leave me, I shall follow. I'll hunt you wherever you go, Jenna, and I shan't care how much noise I make about it. *Everyone's* going to know about it. Do you really want your name and face plastered all over the gutter Press?'

'You wouldn't . . .' she breathed.

'I would.' And the tone in which he said it left her in no doubt that he meant it. 'And don't think the papers wouldn't be interested in our story, Jenna. Some of them—I don't have to spell out their names—will do anything for a really spicy sex-story—you don't even have to be well known. And you'd made quite a name for yourself with that catering business you'd built up—you worked for some pretty high-powered names in the business world. How pleased do you think some of those names would be to find themselves linked with the kind of innuendo some of the sleazier tabloids would dream up in their story of a bride who refused to consummate her marriage...?' He watched her ashen face for a moment, then said quietly, 'I'm not letting you go, Jenna. I don't know what's behind all this, but I do know that until yesterday you were as much in love with me as I was—as I *am*—in love with you. Something happened and I want to know what it was. And if you won't tell me, I'll keep you with me until I do. After that— well, maybe we'll think again.'

'Dair—I've already told you. I've *asked* you—*tell me what happened with Lysette.*'

She looked at him imploringly, but his face was like stone again. He was not going to tell her. Whatever had happened, he was not going to trust her. And until he did, there was never going to be any chance for them.

And then he took her completely by surprise. And what he told her left her stunned, not knowing what to think.

'All right,' he said slowly. 'Since it matters so much to you, Jenna, I'll tell you—part of it, anyway. The most important part.' He paused and she saw him draw in a long, ragged breath. She's still important to him, Jenna thought dully. She still matters. And her misery was such that when he spoke at last she barely took in his words.

'Lysette's dead, Jenna. She died three years ago. All I want now is to forget it—all of it. And start life fresh with someone who can love me as much as I love her. Without questions—without explanations.' His smile was twisted with bitterness. 'I thought I'd found that person, Jenna. But I was wrong, wasn't I?'

He swung away and heaved the two suitcases out of the room, leaving Jenna staring after him, her hand at her throat.

Dead... Lysette was dead. And Dair had been truly saying goodbye to her when she had seen him kiss that photograph.

No wonder he hadn't wanted to talk about it. The pain was clearly still with him. And Jenna felt a deep surge of shame flood through her body.

Slowly, she followed him down the narrow stairs. More than anything else, she wanted to tell him how sorry she was, convey her sympathy, her compassion, the love she still felt for him.

But she knew that it was too late. With the clumsiness of her reactions, her rejection of him, her questions, she had driven him away. And only the fact that he had refused to allow her to end their marriage before it had begun gave her the smallest chance of repairing the damage she had done.

Whether she could ever really do so remained to be seen. But would Dair be taking her back to Devon if he didn't also went to mend the rift between them?

Now, six weeks later, Jenna was no nearer to answering that question. Since their early return home—explained as simple eagerness to start their married life in the place where they intended to spend it—Dair had quietly distanced himself from her. Without saying anything about it, he had removed his possessions from the big double room they were to have shared and withdrawn to a smaller room at the back of the house. Night after night, she lay awake in the wide bed, waiting and wondering, while during the day he left her alone in the house, going out early on estate business, working in the fields and barns, coming in only for meals and spending his evenings in his study on paperwork.

She watched his lean face grow haggard with overwork and strain, and knew that there was nothing she could do about it. And her heart wept for the love she had lost—the love that had never been.

'When are you going to see about starting a business of your own?' Dair asked abruptly one day as they shared their evening meal.

Jenna looked up, surprised by the question. She was beginning to grow accustomed to silence, the occasional polite remark or enquiry that served only to emphasise the gulf between them. For Dair to refer to anything personal, particularly something they had discussed in the days before their wedding, had become rare.

She answered cautiously, afraid of a rebuff.

'I—I hadn't thought about it.' It wasn't quite true. The thought had crossed her mind more than once, with a wistful recollection of the support she had been sure Dair would give her in any venture she cared to undertake. But it had seemed useless to pursue it now. She couldn't really believe that Dair would allow this charade to go on for long. Soon, surely, he must grow tired of it and let her go.

'No? I imagined it would be uppermost in your mind. After all, that's why you wanted to get back to the country—to start your own business, away from the rat race.'

Jenna bit her lip. She knew what he was really saying. But he couldn't really believe that.

'If you're insinuating that I only married you to get out of London, you're quite wrong,' she said coldly. 'There would have been nothing to stop me selling up and moving out of London at any time. I didn't have to get married to do that.'

'Except that you had a partner,' he reminded her. 'Denise struck me as a city girl through and through. And without her capital, you might not have found it quite so easy.'

Jenna felt her colour rise, but she could not deny the truth of his words. Denise would never have agreed to leave London. 'So I married you for some capital?' she asked ironically. 'I hadn't realised I was such an ambitious lady.'

'No,' he said quietly, 'neither had I.' There was a short silence and then he said, 'Look, Jenna, we can't go on like this. All right, so we both made a mistake. Or one of us did. And whatever we expected from this marriage, we didn't get it. But since we're here—well, I've been thinking, and I've come to the conclusion we'd better make the best of it.'

'Meaning?'

'You behave as a wife to me,' he said steadily, holding her eyes, 'and I'll put up the capital necessary to get you started in whatever business you choose to start—locally.' He waited for a moment. 'Well—what do you say?'

Jenna felt the fire in her cheeks. 'A—a wife?' she repeated faintly, and he nodded. 'Dair—I can't——'

'Can't bear the thought of sharing my bed?' he said bluntly. 'Yes, Jenna, you make that painfully clear. Very well, we'll eliminate that aspect of it, since it's so distasteful to you. But in all other ways—as far as any outsiders are concerned—you are my wife. And if you keep to your side of the bargain, I'll keep my distance. Does that satisfy you?'

She hesitated. Just what was he actually proposing? That she should behave—when other people were around, anyway—as if they were a normal, happily married couple. That she should run his house, keep him company when he went out, entertain guests at home. That she should never let anyone else see what a fiasco their marriage really was.

In return, he would help finance her business. He would help her start a new venture that might be as successful as the catering business she had run in London. A venture that might well turn out to be the only thing of value she had left.

And she would at the same time go on living with Dair. She would see him every day. She would know when he was well, when he was ill. She would be his companion through life as they had both promised on their disastrous wedding day.

Until that moment, Jenna had never dared to admit to herself just how important that was. She had never acknowledged that the reason she did not abandon him at the outset was not fear of his hounding her through the country, fear of publicity and gossip. It was because, in spite of everything, she still loved him, achingly, despairingly. Because, even now, she could not bear to be parted from him.

That was why she could not let him touch her, knowing that he still loved another woman—even though that woman was dead. Because she needed him to love her, completely, wholly, excluding all others. As she loved him—even though her love threatened at times to turn to hate.

'Do you want time to think it over?' Dair asked quietly, and she looked up and met his eyes, wondering how they could look at her so coolly, so remotely.

'No. I don't need time.' She lifted her chin a little. 'I'll accept your offer, Dair. And I'll keep my side of the bargain—as long as you keep yours.'

He would never know how she longed to open her arms to him then. But the ghost of Lysette drifted between them. And turned them both to ice.

Now, pausing before she opened the garage doors, Jenna looked around her at the countryside that had become her home. The farm stood on the edge of Dartmoor, with the rolling, bracken-covered hills sweeping away behind the square, grey house. It looked out at the softer landscape towards the coast, with the blue Cornish horizon in the far distance. In the valley, its surroundings softened by trees glowing with the flames of autumn colours, was the market town of Tavistock, where Jenna was already beginning to make friends.

She drove out of the garage and across the yard. Dair had gone out early that morning. With October almost on them, he was busy preparing for the various fairs and markets which were the culmination of the farming year—St John's Fair, the Goose Fair, both held in Tavistock itself, and others that took place further afield. It was at these that the farmers sold or replaced their livestock, and Dair was absorbed in improving his own strains.

Jenna turned her mind to her own concerns. Since that day when she and Dair had struck their bargain, she had been busy searching out her own business, and refurbishing was almost complete now in a small shop right in the middle of the main street of the busy little town. She had decided, after some consideration, to concentrate on flowers; she had always enjoyed working with plants, and the hours would be more regular than catering allowed.

Not that irregular hours would affect the kind of marriage she had, she reflected sadly as she drove through the leafy lanes, past the fire station and over the bridge that crossed the river Tavy to reach the main square. Dair was hardly likely to notice, or care, whether she was there or not. They had grown so far apart in the few short weeks since their wedding, they were almost strangers again.

But not quite. Even though they slept in separate rooms, she was always burningly aware of him, only a few yards away in the night. And this morning they had met unexpectedly in the passage between their rooms, Dair casually wrapped in a towel as he made his way to the bathroom, Jenna still buttoning her blouse as she hurried to the kitchen. Taken by surprise, they had both stopped, Jenna staring at the broad chest she had seen naked only once before, on the morning after their wedding, Dair's eyes drawn almost unwillingly to the swell of her breasts still visible under the unfastened blouse.

The encounter had lasted no more than a few seconds. Then Dair, with a muttered greeting, had brushed past her and disappeared into the bathroom. And Jenna had been left standing, her heart kicking at her ribs and her breath coming suddenly fast and ragged.

Jenna brought the car to a stop rather more sharply than she needed and looked up at the front of her little shop. It had been newly painted, with a fresh sign over the door and she couldn't help feeling rather proud of it. The words *Flower Box*, in gold lettering on a dark green background, stood out elegantly in the steep street and over the door swung a gold basket filled with dark green foliage and the brilliant pink and purple bells of fuchsias. Jenna looked up at it, pleased with the striking effect.

Inside, two men were busy finishing putting up shelves. They looked round and grinned a welcome as Jenna came in, and indicated the freshly painted white walls. The older man, by far the most talkative, put down his tools and prepared for a chat.

'There you are, Mrs Adams, 'tis almost done now. Reckon you'll be able to open soon. Pretty little place, too.'

'It will be when it's filled with flowers.' Jenna smiled at them. 'You've done a good job here—I'm very grateful. I'd never have thought we could have everything ready so soon.'

'Ah, us can work fast enough when us has a mind. And have 'ee found someone to help 'ee, then?'

'I hope so.' Jenna glanced out of the big window. 'In fact, she ought to be here soon. Cindy Curtis. Do you know her?'

'Young Cindy?' The two men glanced at each other and nodded. 'Ah, everyone knows young Cindy. Us all felt sorry for her when the kiddie was born. Liddle girl, if I remember right.' He looked enquiringly at the younger man, who nodded.

'That's it. Tanya, her name is. Started playschool with my Andrew. Red-haired kiddie.'

'Be like her mother, then. And started school! Why, I didn't think young Cindy were old enough—seems like only yesterday I used to see her and her mum coming down the Meadows of a morning...' He was off on a long, rambling tale of reminiscence, and Jenna went quickly through to the room at the back of the shop, knowing that as long as he had an audience he wouldn't stop talking. She was still getting used to the leisurely way of life in Devon; the hurry and bustle of London hung around her like a miasma and she was finding it hard to shake off.

Jenna dropped her shoulder-bag on the table and looked around, noting with satisfaction the big sinks and spacious worktops, ready for flower-arranging. In a corner stood several boxes which contained vases and pots bought last week on a trip to the wholesaler's. While she was waiting for Cindy Curtis, she could start to unpack them.

She had almost finished when she heard the shop door open again and a light, eager voice address the painters. A few seconds later, the door swung open and a small, slender girl with a flame of copper hair entered like a whirlwind.

'Hello! I'm Cindy Curtis—I'm awfully sorry I'm late; my little one fell down and cut her knee just as we were setting out and we had to go back in and wash the dirt out of it and find plaster and everything.' She gave Jenna a rueful grin. 'And I suppose that's scotched my chances of getting the job—you won't want someone whose children are accident-prone. I mean, if I can't turn up on time for an interview, how will I ever manage to get to work?'

'Well, you're the only one who can answer that,' Jenna said. She looked at the bright face and sparkling eyes. 'Why don't you have a coffee and we'll talk about it?'

Cindy accepted with the enthusiasm Jenna was to learn she brought to everything she did, and together they found the kettle and made coffee. Cindy took two mugs out to the painters and the older one immediately engaged her in conversation, plying her with questions about her family until Jenna was obliged to go out and rescue her.

'Sorry, but Cindy and I have quite a lot to discuss and I expect she's in a hurry,' she said firmly, steering the other girl into the back room. 'Does everyone know everyone else around here?'

'Mostly,' Cindy said cheerfully. 'It's still quite a small place, you know, even though there's been a lot of development recently. But there's still a lot of real locals left, so the incomers don't really make much difference... I'm sorry, I suppose you're an incomer yourself, aren't you? Aren't you the new people at Sampford Estate?'

'Yes, that's right.' How long did you have to live here before you were considered 'local'? Jenna wondered. About three generations, probably... 'Now, what sort of experience have you with flowers? And what kind of hours would you be able to manage?'

The two girls talked for about half an hour, at the end of which time Jenna was satisfied that her first impression had been right—Cindy Curtis was the kind of girl she would be able to get along with. Inconsequential she might appear, with her blithe references to a home life that sounded little short of chaotic, but she exhibited a sunny, optimistic nature that appealed very much to Jenna, and the directness of her sparkling eyes indicated an honesty that meant that here, at least, there would be no secrets, no hidden grievances or shadowy sorrows. That was something that Jenna, with her own difficult home life, needed desperately in her work.

And Cindy's references were impeccable. From school, she had gone on to technical college, where she had taken a course in display techniques which had included floral art. She had worked for six months in a flower shop before going on to become a window display girl in Plymouth's leading department store, and had then worked with a funeral director. 'Not a very cheerful sort of job,' she admitted with a wry grin, 'but at least I got to do a lot of wreath work. That was before Tanya came along, of course.' She gave Jenna a quick glance. 'You already knew I'd got a little girl, didn't you? You didn't seem surprised when I mentioned it earlier.'

'Yes, I'd heard,' Jenna said gently, and added, 'You don't have to tell me anything you don't want to.'

'Oh, I don't mind. Everyone round here knows what happened anyway.' She paused. 'Chris and I—were going to be married, you see. Then, a month before the wedding, he was killed in a motorbike accident. We'd just spent the evening sending out invitations, I remember.' Her green eyes looked back into the past. 'I hoped Tanya would look like him. But everyone says she's the image of me.'

'I'm sorry,' Jenna said after a moment. 'Things can't have been easy for you.'

'Oh, they could have been a lot worse. My mum's been great—let me stay on with her, helped with the baby so I could work part time in the supermarket. But I wanted to get back to floristry, so it seemed too good a chance to miss when I saw your advertisement. But maybe mornings wouldn't suit you?'

'I don't see why not.' Jenna had advertised a part-time post, hoping to interest more than one applicant so that the hours could be shared out between them. 'What I'd really like is someone to work afternoons as well, so that there would always be someone here. I need two at any time because of deliveries and in case of illness. But if you'll take on the mornings, that would be fine. What about holidays? I suppose the playschool has terms, like the primary school?'

'Yes, but Mum will have Tanya, just as she always has.' Cindy gave her a quick smile. 'Well, what do you think?' She bit her lip, half grinning. 'I shouldn't ask that, should I? I should go away and wait for you to decide. You're bound to have loads of people after a job like this.'

Jenna laughed. 'But not many with the qualifications you've got, Cindy. Yes, the job's yours—subject to a month's approval on both sides, if you like. But I think we'll get along fine. When can you start? Monday next week? I'm hoping to get the first stock in then and we can make up a really super window display and open on Tuesday.'

'Fine,' Cindy agreed enthusiastically, and immediately suggested several ideas for the window display which confirmed Jenna's impression that she had found the right girl for her new business. Together, they went outside and studied the window, then returned to the back room of the shop to look at Jenna's collection of vases and containers and think what else might be needed. Their discussion was interrupted only by the deep, booming tones of the church clock tolling twelve.

'Heavens, is that the time?' Cindy exclaimed. 'I'll have to go and pick up Tanya. I'll be along on Monday, then, OK?'

She departed in a flurry of tawny curls, calling a cheery goodbye to the two painters, and Jenna was left alone, feeling unexpectedly cheerful about her new assistant.

Jenna stayed for a while, sorting out a few further details, and then left to do some shopping before going back to the farm. She felt a good deal better as she drove back through the winding lanes, and even found herself smiling as she came into the yard. It was going to be good to be in business again, working at a job she loved and running it herself. And it was going to be good to see Cindy's bright, happy smile each morning. Already, Jenna felt that the other girl was going to prove more than an employee; she could well become a friend.

She went indoors and saw a letter lying on the kitchen table. It was addressed to her and she slit it open and sat down on a chair to read it.

It was from Rob Preston, the boy she and her brothers had grown up with. Rob, who had followed her and Dair all the way to the airport, hooting and waving. Rob, who had been her childhood sweetheart and given her her first shy kiss.

He had given up the job she'd suspected he hated, at the local comprehensive school, and was going to set up his own studio, woodcarving—for which he'd always shown a talent—and painting. And he'd been offered a cottage on the moor only a few miles from Tavistock.

'It belongs to a friend from university,' he explained in his letter. 'He inherited it from his grandmother, but he's going off to Australia for a year and wants someone to live in it while he's away. Peppercorn rent and a chance to see if I can really make it on my own—it seemed too good to miss. So—I'll be living almost next door again! And since we've been neighbours for the best part of our lives, what could be better?'

Jenna put the letter down on the table. Rob and Cindy. Two friends, one old and one new. And badly, oh, so badly needed.

Until then, she had not fully realised just how lonely she had been in her new life. Now it flooded over her like a cold, bleak tide. And she put her head down on her arms and wept.

CHAPTER FOUR

'SO YOUR friend Rob's coming to live nearby,' Dair remarked when Jenna told him about the letter. 'Very convenient.'

Jenna felt anger begin to flare inside her. 'If you're insinuating that there's anything between me and Rob——'

'I wouldn't dream of insinuating anything,' he drawled. 'You know the truth, after all.'

'Don't be so pompous!' she flung at him, but Dair went on as if she had not spoken.

'I did think at our wedding that he seemed particularly friendly, but at the time I was still besotted with you. I hadn't realised that you were marrying me for your own, quite different reasons so naturally I never dreamed——'

'Dair, stop it! Rob and I grew up together—he's been more like a brother to me.' Remembering the short period when they had made their first tentative experiments with love, she coloured, and knew that Dair had seen her blush. Reddening more deeply with anger, she went on hastily, 'And if we're talking about why we got married, maybe you ought to look at your own reasons, and be honest about them. Then we might start to make something out of this—this travesty.'

He looked at her from under dark brows. 'Do you really think so, Jenna? Do you really think there is anything to be made of it?'

A bitter sadness welled up in her as she met his sombre gaze. Battling with the threat of tears, she considered his words. Did she really think there was any hope of their ever returning to their old footing, to the love she had believed they shared?

No. Because slowly, painfully, she had come to believe that Dair had never loved her. He had needed a wife for his new life—he'd needed a housekeeper, someone who could accompany him to social functions, someone who would perhaps shield him from the approaches of other women when he really wanted no other woman at all. And he had married Jenna because she had been willing—because she had fallen in love with him.

He was angry now only because he had stopped believing that. Because Jenna, needing to salvage her own damaged pride, had locked her feelings away and refused to reveal them to him. How could she let him know just how badly she was hurt . . . how desperately she still loved him?

But, as long as this situation remained, nothing more could ever be made of the marriage they had turned into a bargain.

'No,' she said, almost too quietly for him to hear. 'I don't believe it, Dair. I don't believe there will ever be anything different for us.'

Picking up Rob's letter, she stood up. The remains of their evening meal lay on the table between them. She began to pile them on to a tray.

'You've got what you want,' she said sadly. 'You've got your farm, your estate, your life. You might at least let me have the same.'

Lifting the tray, she turned away. But she was almost at the door when she heard Dair's voice behind her.

'Very well, Jenna. If that's what you want. But re-member this...' She turned to face him and caught the implacability of his glance, the hard line of his mouth. 'As far as anyone outside this house is concerned, our marriage is perfectly normal. And that's the way it stays. No little...distractions. Do you understand me, Jenna?'

For a moment, she was tempted to hurl the tray and all its contents at him. Something in his face stopped her. A steeliness that left her in no doubt that if she did so, he would throw it straight back. But that wasn't all.

There was a strange tremor just under his skin. A hint of emotion that she didn't understand. And that touched her like the brief, glancing pain of a passing spear.

Quickly, before the tears could fall, she turned and went out of the room.

'So here I am.' Rob dropped his rucksack on the floor and grinned at her. 'Well, what do you think, Jenna? Not bad, is it?'

Jenna looked around the small room. It had ob-viously not been lived in for some time—the old woman who had left it to Rob's friend had spent her last months in hospital and, although the cottage had been kept clean, it had a bleak, cold look. The clutter of ornaments col-lected over a lifetime—glasses won at fairgrounds, cheap figurines dedicated to The World's Best Mum, The Nicest Gran in the World—looked desolate and abandoned. The pictures on the walls were faded, the photographs on the sideboard a motley assortment of sepia prints jostling with recent coloured snaps.

'I'll put it all away,' Rob said, following her glance. 'Someone might want them. But I suppose most of it only had a sentimental value to the poor old dear herself. It all looks a bit sad now, doesn't it?'

'In a way.' Jenna moved across to the sideboard, taking a closer look at the photographs. 'All the same, she had a lot of people who loved her, Rob. Look at all these pictures. They must be of her children and grand-children, and these two of babies look quite new—they could be great-grandchildren. All keeping in touch. She could never have been really lonely.'

'No, I suppose not.' He came to stand beside her. 'Still, if you live that long I suppose you're bound to gather quite a crowd around you. You'll be the same, Jenna—half a dozen kids, a dozen grandchildren, umpteen great-grandchildren.' He gave her a teasing grin. 'I can just see you, matriarch of a dynasty!'

Jenna moved away. She could not tell Rob how un-likely a picture this was. How improbable it was that she would ever have even one child, let alone found a dynasty. For a moment, she was shaken by a powerful mixture of anger and despair. What right did Dair have to impose this life upon her? What right did he have to take away her basic function as a woman?

But almost at once, her anger was replaced by reason. Dair had never refused to make love to her. He had never refused her a child. She knew that even now he would be willing to take her to bed, to make love with all the stormy passion she knew was kept battened down, to give her as many children as she wanted. The refusal was all on her side.

And more than once, burningly aware of his presence in the house, she had been tempted to leave her own bed and go to his. To slip between the sheets, stretch her naked body against his, feel the touch of his skin against hers, let her lips explore as his would explore, to hold nothing back as the desire that tortured her night and day was at last allowed full rein...

'What about Meg?' she asked abruptly, thrusting the tormenting vision from her mind. 'Will she be coming down to see you here?'

Rob's face clouded and he put back the photograph he had been studying. 'No. That's something I haven't told you, Jenna. Meg and I—well, it's all off.'

'All off?' She stared at him in dismay, her own troubles temporarily forgotten. 'But why? What happened? You always seemed so right together. Oh——' she made a quick movement with her hand '—don't tell me, if you don't want to talk about it, Rob. I don't want to pry.'

'No, I'd like to tell you.' He sighed and dropped on to the old-fashioned settee, his long limbs sprawled like those of a comic doll. 'I need to have someone to talk to... Basically, it was about all this.' He waved a hand at the small, cluttered room. 'Meg thought it was a mistake to give up my job and try to go it alone.'

'You mean she doesn't think you can make it? But she knows how talented you are——'

Rob gave a crooked grin. 'Does she? I'm not sure. Anyway, talent's not everything, Jenna. You need an awful lot of luck as well. The right people wanting your things... She's right, it's a risk. But—well, I thought it was one I needed to take. Being offered this cottage decided me. After all, if I fail, I can always go back to teaching.'

'And you mean Meg broke with you because of that?'

'That and other things.' The grin was now almost twisted. 'There was another man—the new Head of Physics. He and Meg came into contact a lot, with her being on the science side, and—well, I suppose they hit it off. Anyway, I could see there wasn't much point in my hanging around. When Dave came up with the idea of this place, I asked Meg if she'd come with me. She said no, so that was it.'

'Was it?' Jenna looked at him thoughtfully. Rob had always been easygoing in his relationships, but only up to a point. Then he could become quite intractable. Was this what had happened with Meg? Had he presented her with an ultimatum she couldn't be expected to accept? Had he demanded that she give up her own job to take this risk with him, regardless of her own feelings on the matter? And what was the truth of her relationship with the 'other man'?

Well, it was none of Jenna's business and there was nothing she could do about it. Rob and Meg were both adult people and must make and live by their own decisions.

'Well, I'm sorry about that,' she said. 'I've always liked Meg and I thought she was just right for you.'

'Practical and full of common sense, you mean,' Rob said wryly. 'All the things I'm not. Yes, I'm sure you're right—but, when it came down to it, she turned out to have too much common sense. Or perhaps just enough to see that she didn't want to shackle herself to a ne'er-do-well like me. Well, don't let's go on about it any more, Jenna. It's over now and I'm starting a new life. Makes two of us, doesn't it?' He uncoiled himself from the settee and came over to her, laying an arm around her shoulders as he looked down into her face. 'Let's hope mine turns out to be as successful as yours.'

Jenna stared up at him and to her dismay felt tears come into her eyes. She turned her head sharply, but knew that it was too late. Rob put a hand under her chin and turned her back to face him. His eyes were concerned.

'Jenna? What is it? What did I say?'

'Nothing.' She pulled herself gently away from him. 'It's nothing at all, Rob. I—I'm just sorry about you and Meg, that's all. Now—why don't we bring some more of your stuff in from the car? Or do you want to start packing some of these ornaments and things away first?'

'No, I'll do that later.' His eyes were still on her. 'Jenna, I wish you'd tell me what's wrong.'

'Nothing's wrong.' She faced him, smiling brightly. 'Please, Rob, don't start imagining things. I'm quite all right. Everything's perfect. Everything. All right?' And she went briskly towards the door. 'Now, if you want me to help we'd better get on with it; I do have other things to do, you know.'

'Of course.' He followed her outside and they began to unload his battered little car. 'All the same, Jenna, I wish you'd promise me one thing.' His voice was serious and she stopped and looked at him reluctantly. 'If there ever comes a time when everything's *not* so perfect, and you need to talk to anyone—well, you'll remember me, won't you?'

She met his eyes and knew that he was still unconvinced. He held her look and at last, slowly, she nodded.

'I'll remember, Rob. And—thanks.' She smiled, a little waveringly. 'It's good to have you near.'

He nodded and touched her arm briefly. And then they went on unloading the car.

> 'Tis just a month come Friday next, Bill Champernowne and me,
> We went across the old Dartymoor, the Goosey Fair to see.
> Us made ourselves right vitty, us shaved and grazed our hair,

And off us went in our Sunday best, behind Bill's
  old grey mare.
Us smelled the sage and onions all the way from
  Whitchurch Down,
And didn't us have a blow-out when us put up
  in the town.
And there us met Ned Hannaford, Jan Steer and
  Nicky Square.
I think that all the world was there,
  At Tavistock Goosey Fair.

The tune of the old song lilted through Jenna's head
as she drove into the town on the October morning that
promised to bring the biggest crowds of the year. Already farmers were driving sheep through the streets to
the market out on the Whitchurch road and families with
children enjoying a day off school were being joined by
visitors disembarking from the coaches that were parked
all along the Plymouth Road. The square was busy with
stalls which were still being erected and set out with
fairings of all kinds, ready for the afternoon, while down
by the Meadows roundabouts, switchbacks and dodgem
cars were receiving their final touches.

'Proper meeting-place, the Goose Fair be,' Jenna was
told by Mrs Endicott, the wife of Dair's cowman, who
came in to do the cleaning. 'People meets each other
there that don't see each other from one year's end to
the next. All the folk come in from miles around, see,
so us all catches up with each other's news.'

'But do they still sell geese?' Jenna asked.

'No, not live ones, any road. 'Tis against the law now,
see. You might find a few ready for the oven, just as a
token, like, but there haven't been real geese sold for a
long time now. And the old market isn't like it was when

I were a maid—only a few farmers bring their sheep in on the hoof now, it's all trucks and trailers. Nothing's what it used to be.'

'It still seems very popular, all the same.' Jenna gathered her things together. 'Cindy told me to be sure to get in early, while the roads were still open.'

'Oh ah, there's still plenty come. I'll be down there myself when I've finished here—maybe I'll see you on one of they old roundabouts.'

Jenna laughed. 'Maybe you will! I don't suppose we'll be all that busy in the shop—I'm only staying open for the look of it. Cindy'll be taking Tanya along, of course, so I'll have to be there until closing time anyway.'

'Ah, well, maybe you and Mr Adams'll be down in the evening.' Mrs Endicott winked. 'Proper romantic it be then, up on that Big Wheel with all the lights twinkling below.'

Jenna smiled and left. Nobody, it seemed, suspected that there was anything unusual about her marriage— even Mrs Endicott, who knew more about their home life than anyone else, had not realised that they didn't share the same bedroom. That was because Jenna was in Dair's room early each morning, making the bed; their explanation that he used the room simply as a dressing-room, or to sleep in one night when he was likely to be called out to a sick cow or for lambing, had been accepted without comment.

Cindy was already at the shop when Jenna arrived, busy making the little buttonholes and posies that they hoped to sell during the day. They had spent the previous evening creating a special window display for the Fair, and Jenna was pleased to see a number of people already looking at it. As she went through the door a mother came out with two little girls, all wearing posies, the children also carrying the balloons Jenna had ordered specially, with 'Flower Box' written on them.

'Hi!' Cindy greeted her. 'I opened early—sold a dozen posies already. I hope all the farmers will be in later for their buttonholes before they go for their goose dinners. Wasn't it a good idea?'

'It certainly looks like it.' Jenna dropped her bag and began to help with the posies. 'Perhaps we ought to have tried taking a stall as well—a lot of people will never make it this far once they begin in the square. We'll think about it next year.'

'By next year,' Cindy said confidently as her nimble fingers worked busily on the flowers, 'we shall have such a marvellous reputation, they'll be beating a path to our door, Goose Fair or not! Just you wait and see. Look—here come some more customers.' She went forward quickly, smiling her happy grin, and Jenna watched her with envy in her heart. Cindy seemed to live in perpetual chaos, yet her sunny nature never seemed to fail her and she never appeared to harbour any bitterness over the harsh treatment life had meted out to her.

The day passed quickly. Cindy's prediction seemed to be promising to come true already, as more and more people, noticing the posies and buttonholes, came into the shop. Some of them stayed to look around and to chat, and Jenna felt that the Flower Box had really begun to make its mark. At lunchtime, as Cindy had hoped, the farmers came down into the town from the cattle market and a good many of them were seen sporting buttonholes bought by their wives; in the afternoon a crowd of grinning youths came in, urged by their girl-friends, and bought posies. Amid a good deal of banter, one or two even dared to wear a buttonhole, but, as Cindy remarked to Jenna afterwards, she didn't think the youth of Tavistock were ready yet for such avant-garde fashion.

'Avant-garde?' Jenna laughed. 'Why, buttonholes went out fifty years ago!'

'Then it's just about time for them to come back,' Cindy retorted. 'Don't fashions always go in cycles? And with this one, we can be right up there in front with the trend-setters—see if I'm not right, Jenna!' She looked at the clock. 'Do you mind if I get ready to go now? Mum said she'd come in with Tanya at half-past two.'

'Of course not. It's good of you to have stayed over. We've been busier than I expected. Though it seems to be slackening off now—and just as well, for we've almost run out of buttonholes.'

'Right, I'll just collect my things.' The doorbell tinkled and Cindy's mother came in with the red-haired toddler who looked so much like Cindy. Huge green eyes stared wide-eyed around the shop and Cindy bent swiftly to kiss her, then straightened up. 'With you in a sec, my pretty.'

'Hello, Mrs Curtis, Hello, Tanya.' Smiling, Jenna knelt to greet the little girl. 'Well, are you going to the Goose Fair? Going on the roundabouts? Or are you too small?'

'She'd be on them all day if she got the chance,' Cindy's mother said with a laugh. 'Roundabout mad, she is, hasn't stopped teasing about it for days.'

'Oh, you won't want a balloon, then,' Jenna said and laughed as the red curls nodded vehemently. 'Here you are, you scamp.' She chose a bright blue one and watched, smiling, as the three went out together. A small, happy family, complete in themselves . . . She caught her breath on a sigh that was half a sob, and turned quickly back into the shop.

There were a few rosebuds left, and some fern sprays. They might as well be made up into buttonholes, though the demand seemed to have slackened off now. Most people would be either in the square or at the fair which had been set up by the Meadows. The street outside, closed to traffic for the day, was now almost deserted. From down in the square came a hubbub of sound: the laughter and chatter of the crowds, the hoarse cries of cheapjacks, raucous music from a steam organ which had been set up on the corner.

Absorbed in her work, Jenna did not glance up at once when the doorbell announced a customer. She finished wrapping the delicate stems in silver foil and then raised her eyes.

'*Dair!*'

He raised his brows. 'Why so surprised? Is there any reason why I shouldn't visit my wife in her shop?'

'No,' she stammered, wishing that her heart wouldn't thump so hard. 'No, of course not—but you never——'

'Never do,' he supplied. 'No. Well, perhaps I thought it was time I did.' His glance fell to the buttonholes she had been making. 'So you're responsible for the whole town looking as if it's at a wedding. An attractive idea.'

'Thank you,' Jenna faltered. She looked at him nervously, wondering why he had come. He had never shown the slightest interest in the shop before, apart from organising the finance for her. Now he was looking around, apparently with approval.

In a casual jacket and open-necked shirt he looked, not conventionally handsome, perhaps, but certainly striking enough to turn a good many female heads as he walked down the street. She felt yet again the heavy sadness that settled over her whenever she thought of the expectations that had turned so sour. Why had he taken such trouble to win her heart? Why had he married her?

Why did he want to stay married to her?

She thought again of the cottage Rob had just moved into, with its clutter of photographs carefully collected and displayed by an old woman with a large, still growing family.

She thought of Cindy and Tanya, facing all the difficulties of the single-parent family, yet happy to be with each other, asking for nothing more.

She looked ahead, into a barren future.

No. She couldn't go on with it. And she gathered together all her courage and faced her husband.

'Dair——'

He picked up one of the buttonholes, a red rosebud with a spray of dark green fern. 'This is a nice one. I'll have it, please.'

Jenna stopped, her words dying in her throat. Stupidly, she looked at the flower in his hand.

'You want . . . a buttonhole?'

'Yes. Why not? This one, please.' His dark blue eyes twinkled a little, astonishingly. 'Is it expensive?'

'Don't be silly!' Her voice sharpened with embarrassment; cursing herself for the tremor that shook it, she searched for a pin to fasten it with. 'Do—do you want to wear it?'

'Of course. Isn't that the idea?' Damn him, he was *laughing* at her! What had got into him this afternoon?

'Dair——' she began again, but once more he interrupted her.

'Well, aren't you going to pin it on for me?'

'Me?' she echoed, and felt her colour rise as he smiled at her. Her skin tingled. It was not the smile she had grown accustomed to, cold and sardonic; instead, for a moment, she caught a glimpse of the old Dair, the one she had fallen in love with, warm and human and vulnerable. She felt a warmth around her heart, an ache in her throat. Oh, Dair, Dair, she thought, what life could have been for us...

'Pin it on for me, Jenna,' he said quietly, and handed her the buttonhole.

With shaking fingers, Jenna took it. He came to stand close beside her and she felt the warmth of his body, the touch of his breath on her cheek. Tears misted her eyes and she blinked rapidly, looking down at the flower in her hand. She had carried roses of just this colour on her wedding day.

Jenna saw the smiling faces of the wedding guests, her father's pride, her mother's joy. She felt again her own happiness, and the pain that had followed.

Was it possible to forget?

'Please, Jenna,' Dair said as she hesitated, and she lifted the flower to his lapel and fastened it on with a quick movement.

They were standing very close, Jenna's hands touching his chest. She could feel his heartbeat beneath her fingers. She looked up and met his eyes, dark as midnight. Slowly, his own hands came up to imprison hers against his breast.

'Jenna...' he breathed, and again she felt the heat of tears.

She dropped her glance at once and tried to free her hands, but he held them too tightly.

'Dair—please. I've got work to do——'

'Nobody's come in since I've been here,' he countered. 'Nobody's going to now. You might as well shut up shop.'

'The buttonholes——'

'Give them away. Put them outside in a box. There are only a few left anyway.' His hands were gripping hers. 'Come with me, Jenna. You've never seen a Goose Fair before. Let me show you the delights of Tavistock making merry.'

He was laughing; he looked ten years younger, a boy out for a day with his sweetheart. Jenna looked at him uncertainly. He tugged again at her hands and she felt her heart lift a little. Perhaps there was hope after all…and even if not, what harm could there be in letting herself be swept along by this new, carefree Dair? If the blackness returned tomorrow, why should she not have just one magical day to remember?

'Lock up the shop,' he urged her, and then, as she turned to snatch up her jacket, 'No—wait a moment.'

There was one white rosebud left. He picked it up and fastened it to her lapel.

'Now let's go,' he said, and bent his head to drop a kiss on her hair.

The October sun was warm in a sky of tender blue. Dair led Jenna thought the swarming crowd. He stopped at every stall, buying home-made toffee, a brilliant silk scarf, a comic little china cat. He drew her past the tall tower of the church, past the few scraps of stonework that were all that remained of the old Abbey, and into the fairground where farmers and their wives, their business over for the day, stood in chattering groups while the roundabouts and switchbacks echoed to the cries and laughter of the children.

'Let's go on the big roundabout,' he said as if he were a small boy, and they climbed on to two golden horses and galloped in undulating circles above the heads of the crowd. They tried the switchback next, gasping as it dipped and rose sharply, and then the dodgems, laughing helplessly as Jenna's car got hopelessly entangled with that of two small boys. Then they came to the ferris wheel, and Jenna felt Dair clasp her hand.

'Well?' he said softly. 'How's your head for heights?'

She wanted to refuse. The thought of being fastened into a flimsy seat with Dair, marooned high above the ground, was more daunting than any mere fear of heights. But the clasp of his hand was warm; the feel of his arm around her on the switchback had been more precious than she had expected. And when she looked up into his face, the expression in his eyes made it impossible to say no.

They joined the short queue waiting for a seat and after a few minutes were strapped in side by side.

As the wheel began its slow progress, Jenna was silent. She was burningly aware of Dair's arm around her shoulders, his body pressing lightly but closely against hers. Her hair was brushing his cheek; if she turned her head, her lips would touch his face. And all the while they were rising slowly, inexorably, higher and higher. Out of the reach of the ground and safety; out of the sight of other people.

'Relax, Jenna,' Dair said in her ear. 'I can't do much to you up here, after all!'

Can't you? Jenna thought frantically. Only make me feel totally helpless, that's all; only turn my flesh to jelly and my bones to water... Oh, why did I ever agree to come on this terrible machine?

She felt Dair's arm tighten about her shoulders, drawing her harder against him. Again, she felt his heart beating strongly against her. The tingle on her skin had spread, aching into her palms, into her stomach, into the soles of her feet. She knew that in a moment he would turn her to him and kiss her, and she knew that she would let him.

'Dair——' she began desperately, and could find nothing else to say. She bit her lip and wished she could stop the trembling of her body.

Dair lifted his other hand. He placed his fingers under her chin. Gently, firmly, he turned her head. He looked deep into her eyes.

'We've started badly, Jenna,' he said quietly. 'I'm not sure whose fault it is—maybe it's mine, maybe we both have hang-ups we can't quite handle. But I think we could handle them better together than apart, don't you?'

Jenna closed her eyes for a moment. She wanted nothing more than to let herself relax in his arms, rest against that broad chest. She shook her head blindly.

'I don't know, Dair. I——'

'I think *I* know,' he said. 'And if you'd only trust me, Jenna... Or even trust yourself. Trust your own feelings—I'm damned sure they haven't really changed.' His fingers shook against her cheek. 'Jenna, this isn't the way I want us to live. It was all so good before. It can't all be gone. Don't you think we can recapture it?'

Jenna opened her eyes and looked into a vivid urgency of cobalt-blue. Her resolve, already weakened by the carefree afternoon and Dair's magnetic presence beside her, failed completely. She yearned for the love they had shared before their wedding day, for the laughter, the kisses, the promise of joy. The loneliness of the weeks since then was too bleak to contemplate.

'Dair...' she whispered, and let her eyes answer his question.

The ferris wheel had stopped with their seat on the very top. Below them, the fairground seethed with people, the music of the roundabouts clashing in joyous celebration. And as Dair's lips met Jenna's, she felt a swell of emotion that was almost terrifying, as if they were both falling through the space in which they swung, as if the wheel, the fairground, the entire town and its ancient celebrations had faded and disappeared, leaving nothing but the two of them, floating high above the earth in a world far removed from bustle and noise.

Dair's lips moved slowly, sensuously, over Jenna's. Gently, tenderly, he shaped her mouth to his, then shifted to plant tiny kisses at each corner, out to her ears, down the quivering column of her neck to her throat. With one hand, he caressed her breast, his fingers moving the fabric of her shirt over her skin with sensual friction. He touched her swelling nipple and cupped the fullness of her breast in one hand as he bent his face towards it.

Jenna lay against him, barely aware of their situation. She felt the tremor as the ferris wheel began to move again and knew a quick stab of agony at the threat that it presented—that they would reach the bottom again, have to get off, have to stop this delicious, this essential lovemaking.

But the wheel moved for only one space before stopping again, and Dair's lips returned to hers. She responded with a hunger that startled them both, seeking his lips with a passion that brought his own rising to meet it. With a sudden desperation, they held each other tightly, straining for an even closer contact. The seat which had been their passport to heaven had now become a confinement, a restricting prison. Oh, let us get down,

Jenna thought longingly, let us find somewhere quiet, somewhere we won't be interrupted...

The wheel began to move again. Dair released her and looked into her eyes. The question there was plain, and she nodded.

'The shop,' she said huskily. 'We can go to the shop.'

The wheel was descending now. Her hand in Dair's, Jenna watched, praying that it would not stop again until they reached the bottom. She stared down at the crowd, the children with candyfloss and coconuts, the teenagers in their jeans, the young men with girlfriends who carried teddy bears and cuddly toys won at the shooting butts.

They were almost at the bottom. The wheel stopped to release the couple before them. In a moment, it would be their turn.

And then Jenna saw her. A woman who stood out sharply from the rest of the crowd, as if she were in Technicolor while everyone else had faded to sepia. A tall, statuesque woman with long blonde hair that shimmered like the finest spun gold. A woman who had gone almost at once, like a passing shadow, but who had been there—who had most definitely been there.

The woman in the photograph Jenna had seen in Dair's hands on the day of their wedding.

The woman who had been his fiancée and who he had said was dead.

Lysette.

CHAPTER FIVE

SHE WAS gone as quickly as she had appeared, vanishing into the crowd. Jenna stared after her, rigid with shock. As the wheel came full circle and stopped again, she turned to Dair, but at that moment the attendant stepped forward and released the bar that had held them in their seat and she was forced to get out.

'Dair——' She caught at his arm and he turned, smiling the slow, warm smile that had once—a few minutes ago, a century ago—turned her heart over and now left her baffled and disillusioned. 'Dair—I don't want to go to the shop——'

'Neither do I,' he said softly. 'Let's go straight home—hm?' And he took her hand in his and drew her after him, through the swarming people.

It was beginning to grow dark. The fairground was alive with lights. Every sideshow twinkled with them, every ride flashed its own enticement. As she looked back, half expecting to see Lysette again, Jenna saw that the ferris wheel was a sparkling circle rising into the sky, slowly moving against the first of the evening stars. More people were arriving and the air was filled with music and laughter. It sounded hollow in her ears.

Dair was leading her away, into the quiet darkness of the Meadows, where lovers already walked beside the narrow canal or, on the far side, the rushing river. The children's playground was silent, the swings idle, unable to compete with the glittering attractions of the fairground. The grass was dry, untouched yet by the heavy dews that foretold warm October days, and a few roses still bloomed beside the path.

'Where are we going?' Still shaken, Jenna found herself hurrying along beside Dair, helpless to sort out her own confusion. How could Lysette be in Tavistock, at the Goose Fair, when Dair had said...? 'Dair, where are you taking me?'

'Home, of course. My car's parked at the other end of the Meadows.' He stopped and drew her swiftly into his arms. 'We can be home in ten minutes, Jenna.'

There was no mistaking his meaning. Heavens, hadn't it been her own desire that had fuelled his? But now... with this new knowledge, how could she allow him to make love to her? How could she accept what she now knew to be a lie?

'Dair—wait.' He looked down at her, and her courage failed her. She could not begin her questions here, where anyone could come along at any moment to hear. 'My car,' she said weakly. 'It's parked behind the shop.'

'We'll collect it in the morning.' He tightened his arms about her and bent his head. 'Don't imagine I'm letting you out of my sight now,' he murmured as his lips touched hers.

Jenna closed her eyes. His kiss was tender, seeking, and she longed to respond to it. For a few seconds, she felt her own lips relax, almost against her will. For a brief moment, she was a part of him, unable to reject the passion she sensed so clearly in his hardening body. And then he pulled away and she had an impression of loss so keen that she almost cried out.

'Not here,' he whispered. 'Not now... We've waited so long, Jenna, we can wait another quarter of an hour...'

He was off again, pulling her with him to the road where his Range Rover was parked. Quickly, he unlocked the doors and Jenna climbed in, still shaken, still trying to sort out her own chaotic feelings. Dair leaped in beside her and started the engine.

They were both silent on the way home, Dair negotiating the twisting lanes with concentration. Jenna held her hands together in her lap, staring unseeingly through the windscreen, trying to come to terms with all that had happened in the last hour or two—ever since Dair had come into the shop and asked for a buttonhole.

Why had he done that? Why had he come to her, as if in truce, as if determined to make peace with her? Was it simply that he was tired of the cold war that had been going on between them ever since their wedding day? Did he simply want a more comfortable atmosphere in his home—and for heaven's sake, didn't she want it too? Or was he sexually frustrated and determined that she, as his wife, should be called upon to ease his feelings? Miserably, Jenna acknowledged that this was probably the case—nothing deeper than a physical need which she was expected to assuage. And at the same time, she was forced to acknowledge that she had her own needs—needs that she could not fulfil with any other man...

The thought that it might be something deeper—something growing close to love—she dismissed at once. She could still not forget the sight of Dair with Lysette's photograph in his hand. And, since that moment on the ferris wheel when she had seen a woman with long hair the colour of ripening wheat, with eyes as green as a mermaid's tail, she could not forget that he had lied to her.

Lysette was not dead. She was very much alive, and in Tavistock. And Dair must—surely he must—know that.

So why his change in attitude?

Perhaps it was *because* Lysette was here. Perhaps he needed to make sure of Jenna, to make her truly his wife... but why?

Jenna shook her head, unable to find an answer. And turned her attention to another, even more pressing question.

What was she going to do when they reached the farmhouse? Because her response to Dair's kisses had proved one fact, and it was one that until now she had found too uncomfortable to face.

It was as if her body refused to be convinced by what her reason knew. However Dair might betray her, she was as much in love with him as ever. And if he were determined to make love to her, she was not at all sure that she would be able to refuse.

Darkness had fallen completely by the time they arrived at the farm and the house lay in a pool of moonlight, its windows gleaming against the grey stone walls. Beyond it rose the dark slopes of Dartmoor, with the rugged shape of the tor standing out against the pale sky. The sound of the stream which ran down beside the house could be clearly heard, and from somewhere in the woods below came the lonely hoot of an owl.

Jenna stepped down from the Range Rover. Inside, she knew, the house would be cheerful and welcoming. Before their marriage, she and Dair had spent a good deal of time in choosing colour schemes for the rooms they had decided to redecorate and now the big living-room, the kitchen and the bedroom they had planned for themselves reflected a taste they had discovered together. Unobtrusive central heating made a comfortable background for the open fires they both loved, and one was always laid in the bedroom, though until now it had never been lit.

As they went in through the kitchen, Dair took a box of matches from a shelf and smiled at Jenna.

'We'll light that fire tonight, my love.'

My love. Jenna closed her eyes against the painful doubts. Did he—*could* he—really mean those words? Or was this all some cynical ploy—a ruse to weld her more closely to him, to make it harder for her to call a halt to the uneasy life they had shared?

Dair was leading her towards the stairs. She drew back, unable to make that final commitment—for commitment it would surely be. Once Dair had made love to her, once she had known at last the joy of being as close to him as two people could ever be, there would be no drawing back. For good or ill, she would be committed to him for the rest of her life.

And he knew it. There was no doubt of that. Already, in his vivid eyes she could detect a tiny spark of triumph. Already he believed she was his...

His to do what? To submit, to be enslaved, controlled?

To stand meekly by while he took up his affair with Lysette? To wait at home while he came and went as he liked?

No. *No.*

Jenna pulled sharply away from him. She freed her hand and backed away across the kitchen.

He turned and stared at her, his brows coming together. 'Jenna? Is something wrong?'

'You know there is,' she said huskily. 'Everything's wrong.' To her annoyance, she felt her eyes fill with tears. 'Dair...how could you?'

'How could I what?' He came towards her, his hands held out, palms upwards. 'Jenna, what's the matter? What's got into you?' He moved quickly, suddenly; before she could evade him, he was close to her, trapping her in his arms. Jenna struggled, but his strength was too great and she found herself held as if by bands of steel. Panting, she stared up into his face and felt the same conflict begin in her again, the desire to melt against him warring with what she knew of the truth.

'What the hell is this?' he said slowly, staring down at her. 'Just what game are you playing with me, Jenna? One minute you're on fire, giving me all the signals—and the next, you're freezing me off again. Or trying to.' He looked closely into her burning face. 'I don't believe you really want me to stop at all. In fact, I'm damned sure you don't. Is this the way you enjoy it, Jenna—the cries of protest, the struggles, the pleading? A sort of sub-rape?' A spasm of emotion twisted his face. 'Well, it's not what I had in mind—I've always preferred the idea of a woman who loves me and doesn't mind showing it, and acting it. The sort of woman I thought you were—but maybe I was wrong about that?'

Quivering with terror now, Jenna shook her head. He hadn't been wrong; she longed to rest in his arms, to respond to his kisses with caresses of her own, to whisper words of love without restraint, without thought of rebuff. To be totally secure...

Security. The one thing she could not be sure of.

Dair was gripping her tightly, his own body trembling. She could feel his muscles, hard against her, throbbing with a passion that drove all the breath from her body as he pulled her towards the stairs again. Feebly she tried to resist, but he ignored her efforts and dragged her through the door and up the first few steps. He was breathing hard, and when she looked up into his face it was like looking at a stranger.

'All right!' he muttered, thrusting open the bedroom door. 'If that's how you want it, Jenna... It's not my idea of the ideal way to consummate a marriage, but I'm past the hearts and flowers stage now.' He flung her across the bed and glared down at her sprawling figure. 'I've had just about enough of your party games,' he growled. 'Living in the same house with you, having to watch you day after day, flaunting yourself at me—now you see me, now you don't, look but don't touch, come close and keep your distance... Don't you realise what that does to a man, Jenna? Don't you understand anything?' His eyes burned and Jenna shivered as she saw his fingers go to his belt. 'Well, maybe you do at that. Maybe you know just what it does—and that's what you like. The idea that you've reduced a man who loves you to a tattered wreck. Maybe that's what excites you—the thought of your own devilish power, and the thought of what you can drive a man to do—as you've driven me now...'

He came close, menace darkening his face, and Jenna shrank away from him, her skin cold with fear, her limbs paralysed. Staring up at him, she could only move her head from side to side, only whisper the words, 'No. Please, Dair, no. *No*...'

'*Please, no,*' he mocked her. 'Don't you mean *yes*, Jenna, my dear? Don't you really mean *please, yes*?' Scorn whipped through his tone as he leaned down and unbuttoned her blouse. 'Well, we'll find out, shall we? We'll find out just what the truth is...'

No amount of protesting would save her now. It was clear to Jenna that Dair firmly believed in what he was saying—that she had been deliberately leading him on, teasing him through all the weeks of their marriage, first seducing and then refusing him in an attempt to drive him into some kind of sexual frenzy. No amount of denial would convince him otherwise, for he had reached a pitch of frustration that was beyond rational thought. Any further refusal would only intensify his furious passion, and Jenna feared what might happen then.

There was nothing for it now but submission.

She closed her eyes and lay still. She could feel Dair's fingers on her clothes, trembling as they dragged her blouse open and pulled away her skirt. Scorched with embarrassment and shame, she lifted her hands to her face, but Dair wrenched them away and held them above her head, one strong hand fastened around both her wrists. He ran his other hand strongly down her body, from neck to thigh, and she quivered and cried out. Instantly, his mouth was on hers.

The kiss was savage. His mouth was harsh, forcing her lips apart, teeth tearing at the soft flesh, tongue thrusting against hers. His hands were ruthless; there would be bruises around her wrists tomorrow, and on her body. Her sobs were forced back into her throat and her body seemed to shrivel beneath his weight.

She had dreamed of this moment, when they lay together at last with nothing between their bodies, nothing to hold them back from that final dedication. But not like this—dear lord, not like this....

Dair lifted his lips from her skin. His hand was moving rhythmically over her body now, cupping and caressing her breasts, stroking her flat stomach, drifting downwards to the silkiness of her thighs. He stared down into her eyes and she could see the moonlight reflected deep in the midnight blue of his. Slowly, he released her hands and his fingers touched her cheek softly, almost wonderingly.

Jenna returned his look. There was a moment of complete stillness. And then he bent his head again and kissed her lips.

His mouth had lost its harshness now, tenderly searching hers, his lips a balm for the bruises his teeth had inflicted. Almost without her knowing it, Jenna's hands wandered to his head, her fingers tangling in the thick, night-black hair, and she lifted herself against him and moaned softly.

'Jenna...' he murmured against the throbbing pulse of her throat. 'Jenna, Jenna, my darling... what have we been doing to each other?'

The tears flowed from Jenna's eyes and soaked into her hair. Why could it not have been like this from the start? Why had it all been spoiled? She had never doubted her love for Dair—why had she doubted his for her? It all seemed so hazy now, so far away. So unimportant, when here they were in each other's arms and the world had ceased to exist. When nothing mattered but themselves and the love they shared.

With exquisite care, Dair finished undressing her. He stretched his naked body beside hers and held her close, and for a few moments they lay quite still, aware only of the tingling of their skin, the rapid beat of their hearts.

At last he raised himself above her and looked down, a question in the moon-shadowed eyes. In answer, Jenna reached up and drew his head down to hers, and in the same moment, smoothly and easily, he slipped into her body.

Later, covered now by the duvet and watching the moon ride slowly across the huge, dark bowl of the sky, Jenna

turned to Dair and asked the question that she knew had
to be answered if the love they had rediscovered was to
endure.

'Dair... please tell me about Lysette.'

And yet again, with horrifying inevitability, his answer
shattered her dreams and destroyed her trust.

'I've told you before, Jenna. Lysette is dead...'

In the short time since he had moved in, Rob had been
busy at the cottage and had already packed all the ornaments and furnishings into boxes, ready to be col-
lected by his friend's father. In their place, he had put
bright cotton rugs and a few of his own paintings and
woodcarvings. The shelves were filled with books and
in the small outbuilding he had set up a workshop and
studio.

'So what's the verdict?' He beamed as Jenna finished
looking around and came back into the living-room
which, though still tiny, looked a good deal lighter and
more spacious than the first time she had seen it. 'Think
I've done a good job?'

'A marvellous job,' she said. 'And I love the work
you've already done. I hope you do really well here, Rob.'

'So do I,' he said with feeling. 'It's a big step, you
know, throwing up a steady career and taking off like
this. Could turn out to be a disaster.'

'Almost as bad as getting married,' Jenna said, and
tried to turn her words into a joke with a chuckle. But
her laughter sounded forced and she turned hastily away
from Rob's sharpening glance.

'You sounded as though you meant that,' he said
quietly after a moment. 'What's wrong, Jenna?'

'Wrong? Nothing. What should be wrong?' In spite
of her efforts to keep her voice casual, there was a high

note to it that quivered. She was aware of Rob coming closer to her, then felt his hands on her shoulders. He turned her to face him.

'You don't fool me, Jenna,' he said quietly. 'I've known you too long. I'm Rob, remember? The boy next door. I've seen you trying not to cry when you've grazed your knee or one of those brothers of yours has hidden your favourite doll, or you've tried a rinse on your hair and turned it green... You can tell me, Jenna, if you want to, or you can tell me to mind my own business. But don't try to tell me there's nothing wrong.'

Jenna shook her head, feeling the tears hot in her eyes. She looked down and saw one fall on to her hand, and knew that Rob had seen it too.

With a sob, she let her hand drop against his shoulder and felt his arms slip round her shoulders to hold her close and comfortingly against him.

'Oh, Rob,' she wept, 'everything's such a muddle. And I can't tell you—I don't really understand it all myself. All I know is that Dair doesn't—doesn't really love me.' And the tears that she had held back for so long over-whelmed her.

'Hey, hey.' Rob led her to the sofa and pressed her gently back against the cushions. He sat down beside her and took her into his arms again. 'That can't be right.' He waited, still holding her, while she wept and snuffled, and finally felt in his pocket and brought out a large handkerchief. 'Jenna, you've got to be wrong. Of course Dair loves you.'

'No,' she said dolefully, 'he doesn't, Rob. Not really.'

'Then why did he marry you, for goodness' sake?'

'I don't know. I just don't know what reason he had.'

'Well, I do,' Rob said forcefully. 'He married you be-cause he loved you. Look, anyone who was at that wedding would tell you the same. It was obvious! You only had to see his face. Surely you believed that, Jenna? You certainly looked as if you did.'

'I thought I did,' she said miserably. 'It was only afterwards that I—that I found out——'

'Found out what?'

'That he was still in love with his first fiancée. Oh, he never made any secret of the fact that he was engaged before—but he's never talked about her, Rob. He still won't. And I saw him with her photograph in his hand, just before we left on our honeymoon. He—he was saying goodbye—and saying sorry to her.' Jenna raised her tear-streaked face. 'He still loves her, Rob, I know he does.'

Rob was silent for a moment, considering this information. Then he asked the question Jenna had been asking herself ever since. 'Then why didn't he marry her? Why should he marry you, if he still loved her?'

Jenna shrugged helplessly. 'I don't know. I just don't know. Perhaps she found someone else after they broke up, and got married herself. If only I knew what had happened, it might help—but I can't ask him. He just won't talk about it.' She paused and blew her nose. 'His Aunt Mickie, who used to look after him, told me never to ask—she said it was too painful for him.'

'So she knows what happened? Why don't you ask her?'

Jenna shook her head. 'She's gone abroad. She has a sister in New Zealand and she decided to go and visit her. It—it's not a thing I can ask in a letter, Rob. It all takes too long, and I think she would just say it's for Dair to tell me when he's ready.'

'So why don't you wait for that?' Rob asked gently. 'Why tear yourself apart over this, Jenna? Dair married you, not her. And I'd swear he loved you—still does. Don't forget, I've seen him too since I came down here—and he still has that look in his eyes when he watches you. Why are you letting it get to you like this? Or—is there something more?'

Jenna managed a rueful smile. 'You're right, Rob, you do know me too well . . . Yes, there is. You see, I did ask Dair about Lysette. And he told me——' she swallowed and then went on '—he told me she was dead.'

'Dead! Then——'

'It could make it worse, couldn't it?' Jenna said quietly. 'There's no rival worse than a dead one. But even that's not all. You see—it isn't true.' She stopped, watching his face. 'I saw Lysette last week—at the Goose Fair. She's as alive as you and I. And she's somewhere near here.'

There was a long silence.

'Yes,' Rob said at last. 'I can see that you've got a problem there. Something's definitely wrong. But—Jenna—none of this would matter if you could be sure he loved you. What ever happened between him and—and Lisa, was it——?'

'Lysette.'

'Lysette—none of it would affect you if you felt sure of him. But you don't, do you?'

'No,' Jenna said. 'I don't.'

'Oh, my poor Jenna,' Rob said, and he put his arms around her again and held her in a warm hug. 'My poor, poor Jenna.'

Jenna rested against him for a while, then pulled herself away and sat upright. She gave her nose a final blow, wiped away the last few tears and lifted her chin. Her mouth was set with determination.

'Thanks, Rob. I needed that—a shoulder to cry on. But I'm not going to do it again.' She turned and looked at him, her eyes the colour of the bracken that swept over the moors around the cottage. 'All right, so my life's a mess—but it doesn't have to go on being one. Whatever's wrong between me and Dair, it doesn't have to rule me. I can make a success of myself some other way—just as you're going to here, with your painting and woodcarving.'

'That's the girl!' Rob said admiringly, his thumbs in the air. 'We're just two slightly battered ships, temporarily adrift in the night—but it's not going to last, is it? We're going to get ourselves together and sail on—and we'll make harbour.' He laughed at his metaphor. 'Not very flattering, but we passed that stage a long time ago, didn't we?'

Jenna smiled waveringly. 'You've been a good friend to me, Rob,' she said huskily, and leaned forward to kiss him, then stiffened. 'What was that? I heard a noise—is someone——?'

Rob laughed and leapt up from the sofa, pulling Jenna with him. 'No, there's no one there, Jenna. Only—well, come and see what I've got to show you! Maybe something like it will be the answer for you, too.'

Wondering, Jenna followed him into the tiny kitchen. This too had been tidied, with fresh crockery on the dresser shelves and plants on the windowsill. The sun streamed in, brightening to gold a jar of yellow chrysanthemums. And in front of the woodstove which kept the kitchen cosy Jenna saw a round basket with a ball of creamy fur curled up inside it.

'Rob—a puppy! Oh, isn't he adorable?'

'She,' Rob corrected her. 'A yellow Labrador. I thought I'd call her Gypsy—what do you say?'

'It's a lovely name.' Jenna was on her knees, stroking the soft golden head. The puppy opened one eye and put out a tongue the colour of the underside of a mushroom to lick her hand. 'Hello, Gypsy, you little darling. Oh, she'll be marvellous company for you, Rob.'

'Well, there is that too,' he admitted with a grin. 'Of course, I really got her as a guard dog.' They both looked at the bundle of fur, soft as a child's toy, and laughed at the idea of her guarding anything more than a rubber bone. 'She will grow, you know.'

'Of course she will. She's gorgeous.' Jenna gave the puppy a final pat and rose to her feet. 'And do you think she'll make an adequate substitute for Meg?'

Rob shrugged. 'Well, it's a start. At least she won't refuse to come with me when I decide to move on. And she won't criticise me for being lazy or tell me I'm wasting my time trying to be a craftsman... There's a lot to be said for a dog, Jenna.'

'I know.' Jenna smiled sadly at him. 'But I don't think it's the answer for me, Rob. I don't think a dog—even a dog as beautiful as Gypsy—will be enough to fill the gaps in my life. They're just too big.'

'So what will you do?' he asked quietly, and Jenna sighed.

'What can I do? I can't leave Dair—you see, whatever's wrong between us, I know I love him. And he doesn't seem to want me to go, though I don't really understand why.' But that wasn't really true; when she thought of the passion that had flared between them, taking them both like a hurricane, she thought she knew just why he wanted her to stay. It might not be love on his side, it might be no more than chemistry, but he wasn't going to give it up now that he'd finally found it. And Jenna knew that she wouldn't be able to give it up either. Already, her body was crying out for his; already, her lips were yearning for his kiss.

'You're in a trap, aren't you?' Rob said. 'I wish I could help.'

'You can. By simply being here.' She smiled at him and touched his cheek. 'I'm glad you came to live here, Rob. I don't know quite what I'd do without a friend to turn to.'

He looked down at her, his open, rather boyish face serious and a little troubled. Then he put up his hand and held hers for a moment against his face.

'I'm glad too. And I wish I could do more. Promise me one thing, Jenna.'

'Yes?'

'Promise you *will* turn to me—whenever you need a friend. Whatever time of day or night it might be. Promise me that, Jenna.'

Their eyes met. She nodded slowly. Perhaps the promise was a little melodramatic—but she had a feeling that she might one day remember it and be thankful that it had been made.

CHAPTER SIX

'OH, CINDY, I'm sorry I'm late. Still felt a bit weak this morning after that awful tummy bug that's been going around.' Jenna grimaced as she hurried in through the door. 'I wouldn't have come in at all if you and Tanya hadn't had it last week, which I suppose makes you immune for a while at least, and if I stay in the back, just making up bouquets I won't—oh, hello, Rob, I didn't see you there! You've had it, haven't you? I don't want to pass it on to anyone else.'

She looked in surprise at Rob, who had been standing beside a tall yucca plant, his hand on its thick stem. 'Are you thinking of buying that?'

'He already has,' Cindy said cheerfully. 'And that's better salesmanship than you realise, Jenna, because he didn't come in to buy anything at all—he came to sell *us* something! These wooden bowls, look.'

'Oh, yes.' Jenna came over to the counter and looked down at the selection Rob had brought. 'I said a few weeks ago we might be able to use these for our displays. And these lovely pieces of juniper root, all gnarled and twisted—you've polished them beautifully, Rob. That big piece will look wonderful in the window. I wouldn't be surprised if we get a few offers for that.'

'Well, perhaps you'd like to have a few for sale,' Rob suggested. 'I was going to take them to the craft shop but if you think there's a market here...'

'Leave us a few and take a few more there, see who does best. But I'd certainly like the big one for the shop.'

Jenna examined the bowls. 'You know, you've really found your niche, doing this. These are really good.'

'Let's hope others share your opinion, then. I need the money. Got two mouths to feed now, you know.'

Cindy looked at him enquiringly, and Jenna explained, 'Rob's got the most enchanting Labrador puppy—she's called Gypsy. Where is she, Rob, out in the car? Why don't you bring her in and let Cindy see her?'

'I'll do that. She's probably ripping the seats to shreds at this very moment, anyway.' Rob disappeared and Cindy turned to Jenna.

'He's nice, isn't he? Says he's living in the cottage out below Pew Tor. Have you known him long?'

'Most of my life. We lived next door to each other.' Jenna smiled as Rob returned with Gypsy struggling in his arms. 'There, isn't she the sweetest thing you ever saw?'

'Oh, she's beautiful!' Cindy reached out for the puppy and cuddled her, burying her face in the soft creamy fur. 'So soft! Oh, I wish Tanya could see her, she loves dogs.'

'Bring her out to the cottage some time,' Rob suggested. 'I could do with a puppy-sitter—it nearly wears me out having to play with her all the time.'

'I'd love to, but we've no car. It's too far for Tanya to walk.'

'I'll come in and fetch you. What about Saturday— do you work then or does Jenna let you have some time off? She's a slave-driver, I warn you!'

Cindy laughed. 'I work in the morning. Mum looks after Tanya then.'

Jenna glanced at their faces and went through to the back room to wash her hands. She could hear them talking for a few minutes more, and then Rob put his head through to call goodbye and she heard the doorbell ping as he went out. A moment later, Cindy came through, looking a little pink.

'I'm taking Tanya to see the puppy on Saturday afternoon. He *is* nice, isn't he? Has he always made wooden things?'

'Only in his spare time. He's a teacher really. Gave up his job to try this.' Jenna hesitated, wondering whether to tell Cindy about Meg, then decided it was none of her business. Cindy was only going to take her little daughter to see Rob's puppy, after all—and if he wanted her to know about his life, he was the one to tell her. 'Let's start the new window display, shall we? I'm dying to try that big juniper root.'

The two girls worked all morning, fashioning the new display in between selling fresh flowers and making up bouquets and arrangements for delivery. They had quickly realised that this was where Cindy was invaluable—she knew the area so well that she could be out doing the deliveries in half the time Jenna took. And it was convenient for her to do the deliveries in the afternoons, taking Tanya with her.

Jenna worked thoughtfully that morning, mentally comparing her circumstances with Cindy's. On the face of it, she supposed that most people would consider her the more enviably placed of the two. She had a beautiful home, an attractive husband who ran his farm with efficiency and earned a high income, and her own business. She could afford a good car and nice clothes. Yet what did all that really count for? And how did it compare with what Cindy had—a daughter who loved her and gave her real purpose in life?

If Dair had really loved Jenna, she would have believed herself to be the happiest woman on earth. Without it . . . she must surely rank among the saddest.

Jenna shook herself sharply. That was self-pity, and she'd made up her mind to have nothing to do with that. She'd made her decision, and she would live with it—as cheerfully, if possible, as Cindy lived with the problems of being a single parent.

Jenna's decision had been made over and over again, in the silence of the night after Dair had fallen asleep. He had kept his word and moved back into the big bedroom, sharing her bed with a grim determination that almost broke her heart as she contrasted it with the joy she had anticipated. And he made love to her, almost as if in savage revenge, which changed, invariably, to passion. A passion that could have been tender if he had not flung himself away from her in bitter despair when Jenna, grasping at the hope that this time it must be real, gave herself with a response that was almost frightening.

'Hell, what are you doing to me, Jenna?' he ground out one night, his head turned away from her on the pillow. One fist clenched the bedclothes, the other beat at the wall above his head. 'What am I doing here? I come to tame you, to try to find out just what's going on in that beautiful head of yours—and you do it again, night after night, you get into my blood and drive me crazy. What is it about you? What in hell's name is it? Are you some kind of she-devil?'

Jenna's eyes filled with tears at his words. For a few moments she had once again believed that they might this time find true happiness together, the happiness that came when two people were completely united in mind, heart and body. It had been almost within their grasp, she had been convinced of it—and then it had eluded her again, slipping away like a shred of morning mist, as insubstantial and as impossible to trap. And instead, there was this—this helpless rage, this bewildered despair.

She lay staring into the darkness, wondering once again why she let it go on, this charade they were playing out. Why didn't she simply leave, live her own life once again? She didn't need a man as a meal-ticket and she was self-sufficient enough to live quite happily alone. She had done so for several years, after all, and no doubt could do so again.

But hard on the heels of that thought came another—the thought that always hit her when she considered leaving Dair. She *couldn't* live happily alone now. Not now that she knew him and loved him.

She couldn't live without him. But could she really hope to live with him?

Suppose they had a child? she wondered occasionally, and knew at once that it must not be allowed to happen. Children should be the result of love, not of this desperate coupling that seemed to be a striving for something she couldn't name. Children should come into the world with parents who trusted and cared for each other. They shouldn't be used as weapons.

Jenna longed for a child, longed with a hunger that was only a little less than the hunger she felt for a sign of real love from Dair. But until things were right between them, she would not risk becoming pregnant. And it didn't seem that things between herself and Dair were ever going to change.

'Dair,' she said into the darkness, 'why won't you tell me about Lysette?'

She felt him stiffen beside her.

'I've told you all I'm going to tell you.'

'The truth,' she pleaded, and gasped as he suddenly reared up in the bed and swung over towards her. He leaned over her, his eyes glittering in the faint light from the autumn sky, and she cringed at the anger in his face.

'Dammit, Jenna, I *have* told you the truth! Why do you keep on about it?' He glared at her. 'Look, if I hadn't told you the truth, do you think your nagging would force me to now? Leave it, Jenna—give it a rest. I want to *forget* it, the whole thing.'

He slumped back, breathing hard, and Jenna knew he was right. She ought to leave it alone. Constantly nagging wasn't likely to bring her the truth. But she couldn't do it. She had to know.

'And if I told you I'd seen Lysette?' she said at last, very quietly. 'If I told you——'

'*What?*'

'If I told you I've seen Lysette. In town—in Tavistock—what would you say then, Dair? Would you still tell me she was dead?'

He was up again, bent over her, his fingers cruel on her naked shoulders. He lifted her against him, his shadowed eyes searching her face. Then he dropped her back on her pillow.

'I'd say *you* were the one who was lying,' he said tersely. 'It's impossible. You can't have seen her. Because Lysette is dead. Dead. Do you understand? This obsession is getting past a joke.' He thrust himself away from her and out of the bed. 'You ask me why *I* keep lying—maybe I should be asking the same thing. Only I don't really need to, do I? Do you know what I think, Jenna? *Do you?*' He leaned over her, his hands pinning her shoulders to the bed, and she stared up at him, terrified. 'I think all this is nothing more than the product of your own guilty conscience. Yes, I thought that'd hit home! Did you really think you could get away with it in a place like this, where everything you do is noticed? Did you really think I'd believe that it was mere co-incidence that your old lover should just happen to have a friend who could rent him a cottage so conveniently isolated, yet close enough for your clandestine visits? And did you really ever think I'd be fool enough to be diverted by your wild accusations about *my* infidelity, when all the time you were—were——' His face twisted suddenly as if he couldn't bring himself to say the words, and he thrust himself up, away from her.

Jenna lay staring at him, her mind whirling.

'Rob?' she breathed at last. 'You're talking about *Rob*? Dair, how can you possibly think——?'

'I'll tell you how,' he said grimly. 'I happened to be passing that cottage of his one day and I saw your car outside. I came to find you—we'd quarrelled and I wanted to see you, I wanted to try to make it up, for heaven's sake. I glanced through the window as I passed it and realised at once I'd be superfluous to require-ments. Playing gooseberry, I believe is the term for it. You were canoodling with him on the sofa, Jenna. I saw you with my own eyes, so don't try to deny it.'

Jenna was silent. She remembered that day when she had confided in Rob. The sound they'd heard and as-sumed had been made by the puppy. She felt a wave of scarlet brush her face.

'So don't ask me any more about Lysette,' Dair said coldly. 'I'm going to the other room.'

He was gone with a rush of cold air from the doorway. Jenna lay quite still, staring after him. Then she flung herself over in the bed and burst into a storm of weeping.

The bed was cold and empty without Dair. And the rest of the night was long.

* * *

She was still in the window, putting the finishing touches to the display while Cindy made up a flower arrangement in the back room, when a shadow fell across her as someone paused outside to look in.

Jenna glanced up, a smile on her lips. But the smile froze and died.

There, within a yard of her, separated only by the thick pane of glass, stood the woman Dair had told her so positively was dead. The same tall, shapely figure. The same long, blonde hair, the same green, challenging eyes. They looked into Jenna's and Jenna was instantly convinced that they were laughing at her.

Jenna felt her body grow cold. The world spun and fell away. She was conscious of nothing but the woman outside, and a roaring in her ears that sounded like the sneering laughter of a menacing crowd. She swayed and put out a hand, grasping at the juniper root that Rob had brought only a few hours earlier.

The hard wood under her hand brought her back to her senses. With a swift movement, she was out of the window and pulling at the door. As she ran out on to the pavement, she almost collided with someone coming in, but it wasn't Lysette; almost roughly, she pushed the newcomer aside and stared up and down the steep street, busy now with shoppers.

The woman—Lysette—had disappeared. There was no sign of her in either direction.

Jenna stood breathing quickly. Then she turned and went back into the shop, apologising to the customer she had pushed aside, and going straight to the back room to ask Cindy to attend to her.

'I'll be out in a minute,' she said, conscious of Cindy's surprise. 'I'm sorry—I just felt rather faint for a moment—needed some fresh air.' And she sat down on a chair and rested her head in her hands.

Had she imagined it? *Could* she have imagined it? Was Dair right, and it was an obsession that was getting the better of her?

She shook her head. No. The woman had been as real as Cindy. And she had been, unmistakably, unarguably Lysette.

What was she doing here, in Tavistock? Had she known that Jenna ran the Flower Box? Had she come on purpose to taunt her? And did Dair, in spite of all that he said, know she was in the area?

He knew, after all, that she wasn't dead...

Jenna sat quite still in the little back room, listening to the murmur of voices from the shop as if they were sounds from a distant world. And she felt a shiver of menace creep over her body, enclosing it as if with a thin sheen of ice.

Autumn had disappeared in a sudden November storm which whipped the last brown leaves from the trees and sent them whirling across the grass of the Meadows where Jenna had taken to wandering at lunchtime. She took her half-hour early, before Cindy left to collect Tanya from playschool, and made it a rule to leave the shop during that time to enjoy the fresh air.

There was certainly plenty of *that* about today, she reflected as the gusts snatched at her skirt. Winter seemed to be on its way; heavy clouds were building up on the skyline and there was more than a touch of ice in the air. The mothers and small children often to be seen around the swings were absent and the only person to be seen was at the far end of the path which ran beside the canal.

Jenna crossed the grass and came to the river which tumbled on its restless way to join the Tamar just above Plymouth. The storm had increased its size quite dramatically, and the water rushed over rocks and boulders, wrenching at tree-roots which had felt their way down the banks during years of growth. A small brown and white bird bobbed and curtsied on a rock in the middle of the torrent, and then dived in. A dipper, Jenna thought, marvelling that such a tiny creature could survive in the tumult, and she watched until it surfaced again and hopped out on to a rock, shaking its feathers.

Her half-hour was almost ended. Cindy would be glancing at the clock, eager to get off and collect Tanya. Jenna turned and walked back across the grass.

The other person had come nearer, still walking beside the canal. As Jenna came nearer, she turned towards the little bridge which crossed the canal to the path which went through the rose garden to emerge on Plymouth Road. And Jenna realised that it was Lysette.

She stood quite still, then hurried forward. Her only thought was to stop the woman, to say—what? She had no idea, but she knew that this suspense must not go on. As Dair had said, it was becoming an obsession. She could think of nothing else. She saw Lysette wherever she looked, only to realise that she was invariably mistaken. But this time...surely, this time...

The woman's blonde hair streamed down her back. It must be. It had to be.

By the time Jenna reached the bridge, the blonde woman had gone through the gate leading to the road. There were cars parked along it and mothers were collecting their children from school a little further along the road. The blonde woman turned away, walking along the pavement. She was fumbling in her bag.

Jenna broke into a run. She came out of the gate in time to see her quarry stop beside a car and unlock the door. She slid inside and the door slammed shut.

'Oh—please wait, please!' But Jenna's words were lost in the roar of the car's engine. And as she ran up behind it, it drew away from the pavement and accelerated along the road.

Jenna stood staring after it, feeling more than a little foolish. She caught the curious glances of one or two mothers, walking home with their children. She turned away and went slowly back to the shop.

But she had gained some knowledge, at least. She knew that Lysette was still in the area. And she knew what kind of car the other woman drove.

A brand-new, bright red Lotus Elan.

It would be easy to look for it again.

But she did not see the car, or its owner, again for some time and she began to think that Lysette wasn't staying in the area after all. Perhaps she had simply come on a visit—visiting Dair? a niggling whisper asked in Jenna's mind—and had now gone away again. But something told Jenna that the other woman would be back.

Meanwhile, she tried to forget her unhappiness in her work. The shop was doing well now and she and Cindy were already preparing for Christmas. They had made holly wreaths and a variety of fir-cone decorations to hang in the window and around the shop, and Rob's juniper root was now festooned with scarlet ribbon and shimmering glass balls.

He had brought other pieces too and was becoming quite a frequent visitor in the shop, renewing the stock of bowls and polished wooden eggs and carved animals which were displayed on a side table and attracted a good

deal of interest from people who had come in to buy
flowers and plants.

'Rob seems to be doing quite well,' Jenna remarked
one morning just after one of his visits. 'His venture's
paying off. I'm glad—I don't think he could ever go
back to teaching now.'

'No, he needs to be free.' Cindy was busy making an
arrangement to take to a local nursing home and her
face was turned away from Jenna, who glanced at her
speculatively. Since Rob's invitation to Cindy to take
Tanya to visit him at the cottage, Cindy had been sur-
prisingly reticent about him. Yet Jenna was sure there
was an attraction on both sides.

However, if Cindy didn't want to talk about it, there
was nothing Jenna could do. And she had too many
problems of her own to worry too much about the other
girl's.

Jenna and Dair seemed to be living their days now in
a state of armed neutrality. They circled around each
other like two suspicious dogs, each watching the other
for any sign of either aggression or submission. They
ate breakfast together, scarcely speaking as Dair skimmed
quickly through the newspaper, and shared dinner at
night with a polite discussion of the day's events. Jenna
felt that her nerves, stretched as thin as a spider's silk,
would soon snap, and she was relieved when Dair left
the table with a murmured excuse and went to his study
for the rest of the evening. Or even left the house
altogether, striding off across the moors with his dog at
his heels or driving away in the Range Rover to return
late and still silent.

How long can we go on like this? she asked herself in
despair. There wasn't even the chance now that they
might come together, emotionally as well as physically,

in bed. After a month of the intense lovemaking, sometimes savagely passionate, sometimes heartbreakingly tender, which had left Jenna shaken and bewildered, Dair had returned to his own room. He had said nothing, only looked down at her with an unfathomable expression in his dark eyes one night, and then left her. And Jenna, hearing him close the door of the smaller room, had turned her face into her pillow and wept.

Their lovemaking had been painful, an emotional torture which had threatened to tear her apart. But at least she had been able, for a short time each night, to hold Dair in her arms, feel his body warm and tender against hers, and pretend that everything was all right, that their marriage was normal and real and as happy as she had believed it would be. At least she had been able to give him the love that still ached in her heart— even if he had never recognised it.

Watching Cindy now, her fingers busy with the flowers, Jenna felt suddenly restless. She wanted to get out of the shop and be on the move, it didn't matter where. Anywhere so that she didn't have to look at the same walls, see the same faces going past the window, exchange the same remarks with customers who came in...

'I'll do the deliveries today,' she said abruptly. 'There are quite a few for this morning, aren't there? I'll take them now, it'll save you doing them after lunch.'

'Well, if you wouldn't mind...' Cindy said. 'I have got rather a lot to do today. Mum's not well and she needs some shopping.'

'I'll go now,' Jenna said, impatient to be out. 'You've finished that arrangement, haven't you? Where are the others to go?'

'Two to the nursing home, one to Mrs Brownfield at Whitchurch, and one to a cottage near Sampford Spiney—a *Ms* Duran. I don't know her, I think she's come here recently. The cottage was sold after the old man died.' Cindy helped Jenna carry the flowers to her car. 'I'm sorry, I shouldn't have accepted that one for delivery, it's outside our usual limits, but it came over the phone and I didn't realise how far it would be until it was too late—wasn't thinking, I'm afraid.'

'It's all right. I feel like a drive.' Jenna stowed the bouquets and arrangements on the back seat. One day soon she would need to think about a van. 'I'll be back in time to open up after lunch.'

'All right. See you tomorrow.' Cindy turned to go back to the shop, and Jenna started the car and set off towards the nursing home.

There had been a frost overnight and it still lingered in sheltered spots as she drove out of the town on the Whitchurch road. Mrs Brownfield lived up one of the lanes leading from the road to Whitchurch Down—the edge of Dartmoor. At the top, Jenna could see the gate leading to the moor, with a couple of ponies grazing on the other side. From the front of the house she could look out across the valley, past the ruined farmhouse where Francis Drake was born, and away towards the Cornish hills. It was quiet and peaceful in Mrs Brownfield's garden and for a few moments she could almost believe that the peace extended past the bare hedges, across the valley and over the whole world.

But it didn't. It didn't even get as far as her own home.

Sadly, Jenna returned to her car and drove down the lane, turning left at the bottom to drive through the straggling village of Whitchurch and up past the church itself on to the moor. Here, the views were wide and spacious; she drove past a small herd of ponies, a flock of sheep and a few walkers with rucksacks and sticks, before plunging into the deep-cut, winding lanes that led to the village of Sampford Spiney.

Cindy had given her precise directions as to how to reach the cottage, which stood a little way away from the village itself, and Jenna found it standing at the end of a rough track. Thinking that it would be difficult to turn at the end, she decided to leave her car by the road and walk the few yards to the cottage. She took the bouquet from the back seat.

Cindy was certainly good at making bouquets, she thought, picking her way carefully between the ruts. This must be one of the best she had ever done. It was one of their most elaborate and costly ones and in Jenna's opinion looked out of place in these rural surroundings; much as she enjoyed making up bouquets of exotic blooms, her own preference was for a simpler style of floral arrangement. She wondered what Ms Duran was like, to have such expensive flowers sent to her, and why she should be living in such a remote spot.

The cottage was small and plain. It was obviously very old—once a farm labourer's cottage, Jenna guessed—and its slate roof was in need of some repair. The walls were almost invisible under a mass of creeper and ivy, though some had been pulled away from the downstairs windows to let light in. Around it, the small garden was neglected and overgrown, a mass of despondent, dying vegetation.

It looked empty, and Jenna shivered a little. Who would want to live here through the winter? she wondered. In summer, it could be idyllic—but in the short days of December it must be almost unbearably lonely.

She knocked on the shabby door and waited, half convinced that there was nobody here and the telephoned order must have been either a mistake or a hoax.

And then, glancing round her with some uneasiness, she noticed a large shed beside the house, set back and almost surrounded by thick, heavy shrubs. From the tracks that led to it, she could see that it was being used as a garage. She went over to it and peered through a crack in the door—and her heart leapt.

Inside, was a red car. A brand new Lotus Elan. The same car that she had seen only two or three weeks earlier, with Lysette at the wheel.

CHAPTER SEVEN

'CAN I help you?'

The voice, light and pretty with a note of amusement rippling through it like a bright stream through meadows, brought Jenna jerking round, her heart in her mouth.

Feeling herself flush hotly, almost as if with guilt, she stared at the woman who had come out of the cottage and now stood before her, as exotically out of place as the bouquet Jenna had brought.

'Were you looking for someone?' she asked again, and her eyes smiled as they travelled slowly over Jenna in the dark brown corduroy trousers and yellow sweater she wore for work. Almost as if unconsciously, her own red-tipped hands smoothed down the scarlet silk of a dress that looked more suitable for a cocktail party than for a morning on Dartmoor, yet which managed all the same to make Jenna feel dowdily underdressed.

Jenna's heart was beating hard and there was a roaring in her ears as she faced for the first time the woman she had seen in Dair's photograph, the woman she believed to be Lysette. And as she gazed, her last faint hope vanished.

Until now, reason had told her she could, just, be wrong—that the woman she had seen merely resembled Dair's former fiancée, that he had told her the truth when he said she had died. Now, looking into the smooth face with its amused expression, she let that last shred of reason go. This *was* Lysette.

The glinting, emerald-green eyes went to the bouquet Jenna was holding. 'Flowers? Are those for me? Oh——' Her expression cleared. 'You must be from the little flower shop in Tavistock. Oh, how sweet of you to come all this way!' She stepped forward and reached out for the bouquet. 'How lovely.'

'You—you are Ms Duran?' Jenna found her voice at last. 'We—we don't usually deliver this far out—my assistant took the order before she realised——' She stumbled into silence. There was so much she wanted to say—questions she needed to ask—but the words died in her throat. Maybe because, deep down, she still didn't really want to hear the answers.

'Yes, that's my name. And you're——?'

It wasn't possible that she didn't know Jenna's name. She must know that, and more about her. Dair must have told her... A tiny spark of anger flared somewhere deep inside as Jenna stared into the mocking face.

So it was funny, was it? *She* was funny? Well, she'd soon see about that.

'I think you know my name,' she said coldly. 'I'm Jenna Adams. Dair Adams' wife. And you're Lysette Duran.' She paused deliberately, watching the sudden flicker of surprise in the other woman's eyes. Had she really thought that Jenna didn't know...? 'I think it's time we had a talk,' she added, and lifted her chin a little.

Lysette hesitated for a moment and then laughed. 'Well, of course! Why not? It seems we have rather a lot in common. Let's go inside, shall we, out of this cold wind?'

Her lips twitched again and Jenna felt her fury grow. She actually seemed to be *enjoying* this! The beautifully made-up face was full of laughter, as if there were some private joke which was amusing her hugely.

But Jenna was in no mood to be the butt of someone else's humour. Seething, she followed the other woman, unable to help noticing the swirl of the red silk dress and the shimmer of blonde hair that fell loose upon its shoulders. She felt suddenly conscious of her own plain clothes and the more discreet make-up which had until this moment seemed more suitable.

Suitable! What was the point of being *suitable*, when women like Lysette Duran could swoop in like gorgeous butterflies and make everyone else look drab...?

The cottage was better inside than out, its interior recently redecorated and cosily furnished, though it still didn't seem to suit Lysette's flamboyant beauty.

Only a few items—a set of delicate bone-china cups, some elegant wine glasses set out on a side table as if ready for a cocktail party, half a dozen pretty cushions scattered on the old-fashioned armchairs—looked as if she might have brought them to add her own touch of sophistication to the rusticity of her surroundings.

As if, Jenna thought with a sudden leap of hope, she only intended to stay for a short while. Like a bird of paradise, perching momentarily on some jungle tree...

But the hope died as quickly as it had been born. Hard on its heels came another thought.

If Lysette didn't intend to stay in this cottage long, where did she mean to go next?

To Dair?

'Coffee?' Lysette asked, still smiling, and Jenna shook her head.

'No, thank you.' She stood upright, very straight, facing the woman she believed to be her rival. 'I just want to ask you some questions. First of all, you *are*

Lysette Duran, aren't you?' She didn't know why she had to ask that, except that there was still a part of her pleading for this all to be some inexplicable mistake. She looked into the green eyes and they looked back, laughing.

'But surely you've already made up your mind about that? And aren't the flowers addressed to me?'

'Ms L. Duran. Yes.' Jenna spoke dully, sadly. So it was all true. And everything Dair had told her, a lie. And now she knew for certain why he had been so strange lately; why he had avoided her eyes, why he had gone off for hours at a time and refused to explain where he went. 'You were engaged to my husband,' she said flatly.

'Dair? Of course—hasn't he told you all about it?' There was an odd note in the other girl's voice, a note Jenna couldn't quite analyse. 'Perhaps not—he was always a very private person, my Dair.'

Jenna's anger surged. '*Your* Dair? Might I remind you he's married to *me* now? He's not *your* Dair any longer—he's——' She stopped abruptly, unable to say *he's mine*, and saw amusement flicker again in the emerald eyes.

'Is he not?' Lysette said softly. 'Can you be quite sure of that—Jenny, is it?'

'Jenna. But you can call me Mrs Adams.' Jenna felt a spurt of pleasure at being able to say that, but her pleasure was short-lived. Here in the tiny cottage, with December bringing a dark chill to the moor outside, she felt at a bitter disadvantage. She might have the name, the status and all that went with them—but Lysette had Dair's love. And that, she realised sadly, was the only thing really worth having.

'What are you doing here?' she asked quietly. 'What do you want?' But even as she spoke the words, she knew what the answer must be.

Lysette's fine eyebrows arched. 'What do you imagine I want? I want what's rightfully mine, of course—Dair and all that he promised me. It was a mistake, his marrying you, Jenny. He knew it from the beginning, but being Dair he felt he had to try to make a success of it. Well, *you* know his sense of honour.' She laughed, as if Dair's sense of honour was some amusing foible, a joke between them. 'He realises now that it'll never be any use, of course.'

'What do you mean?' Jenna breathed, and Lysette's eyes opened wide.

'You mean he hasn't mentioned divorce yet? Oh, I'm sorry—I shouldn't have said anything. He's waiting for the right moment, I suppose—so sensitive. But perhaps it's just as well. You had to know some time.' Her smile was almost sympathetic. 'It can't really come as a surprise, after all.'

Jenna wanted to say that it did, that there had never been any hint of such a thing between herself and Dair. But she couldn't. It was true that divorce had never been mentioned—but now, seeing her situation more sharply than ever before, she had to acknowledge that it couldn't have gone on for much longer. There was no communication between them now—nothing but a savage, tormenting desire that refused to die, a desire she saw in Dair's face in unguarded moments and which brought a swift flame of response in her own body.

A desire they both fought every day. So that it was almost a relief to be apart.

'You see?' Lysette said softly. 'You knew it had to happen. And really, don't you think it would be better if it happened quickly? A clean break? Better for you—and for Dair? I imagine you still have some feeling for him, after all.'

Jenna turned her head abruptly, blinking away the tears. Some feeling! She knew that the love she had felt for him from the first had never died—it had grown, increased, until her whole body ached with it, until she yearned for his presence, his touch, his kiss. She couldn't live without him—but neither could she live with him. Not as things were now.

Lysette was watching her.

'You know I'm right, don't you?' she said, still in that same soft tone. 'You know it's all over for you and Dair. Why not admit it, Jenny—why not just slip away now, out of his life, and let him come back to the woman he really loves? Let him have the happiness he deserves...'

The happiness he deserves... The implication of her words was clear. That's what you'd do if you really loved him, Lysette was saying. As things are now, he's just miserable—and you can't want that, can you?'

No, Jenna answered silently, I don't want that. I do love him. I do want his happiness. But...she turned back and looked at the woman who stood before her, so stylishly dressed, her face carefully made-up, her hair shimmering with an artlessly casual look that Jenna knew must take hours to achieve, and she wondered. Was this really the woman he wanted, the woman who could bring him that happiness? Would Lysette ever fit into the life of a Dartmoor farmer?

'Dair's rather more than a simple country bumpkin, you know,' Lysette observed, evidently reading her thoughts. 'He's an extremely sophisticated man. He enjoys the cultural life as well. Or perhaps you didn't know that, Jenny?'

Her patronising tone and repeated use of the nickname Jenna hated brought fresh anger scorching suddenly through Jenna's body, and she stepped forward, her back taut, head up, eyes igniting.

'Yes, as a matter of fact I did know. Dair and I met in London—I used to have my own business there too. We went to theatres and concerts—we enjoyed the "cultural life" together. I'm surprised he's never mentioned it.'

'Oh, we have *much* better things to do when we're together than discuss your courting days,' Lysette said swiftly, and Jenna closed her eyes momentarily to hide the pain in them. Was there nothing she could do to puncture the smooth complacency of this poised and confident woman?

'I think I'd better go,' she said. 'There's nothing to be gained by staying here.' She turned towards the door.

'Nothing,' Lysette said behind her, and even though Jenna couldn't see her face there was no mistaking the triumph in her voice. 'And there's nothing to be gained by staying with Dair either. You might as well give in, Jenny—cut your losses and get out. Before you get hurt any more.'

I couldn't be hurt any more than I am now, Jenna thought, walking to her car. But her pride would not allow her to betray that fact to Lysette. And as she reached the end of the short, rutted track, she turned once more and let her eyes look directly into the glimmering emerald of the other woman's.

'Once again,' she said coldly, 'my name isn't Jenny, it's Jenna. To my friends. And to my family. *And that includes Dair.* He's *my* husband, Ms Duran. And until that situation changes, I'd advise you to be a little less sure of yourself. Divorce without consent still takes a very long time, you know. And you are rather assuming I'll consent, aren't you?'

Without waiting for a response, she pulled open the door of her car and slid inside. And as she accelerated away, she had the satisfaction of seeing Lysette's face in the mirror, staring after her. Perhaps her complacency had been punctured after all.

But Jenna's satisfaction didn't last long. As she drove back across the moor, she forced herself to face the fact that if Dair really wanted out, she wouldn't be able to stand in his way. Life with a man who was hankering after another woman was no life at all. And if you loved him as Jenna loved Dair, it could be nothing short of hell.

A hell that had already begun for her. A hell which increased to an almost unbearable pitch when she came down off the moor and caught a glimpse of Dair's own red Range Rover, moving along the upper road in the direction from which she herself had just come. Towards the tiny village of Sampford Spiney.

Towards Lysette.

By evening, Jenna had made up her mind. The situation between herself and Dair must not go on any longer. There could be no more hiding the truth. And surely, now that she had actually met and talked with Lysette, Dair wouldn't persist in the lies he had been telling her.

Lies! The word brought a sob to her throat and an unbelieving shake to her head. Once, not so long ago, she would have staked her life on Dair's honesty, his integrity. She would have gone to the gallows protesting his honour. Even in the past few weeks, she had fought day and night against the steadily mounting evidence of his betrayal, and she had pleaded with him for the truth.

But he had told her lies.

Oh, Dair, Dair, she thought in anguish, how could you do it? How could you deceive me so—and why? When you must have known that Lysette wouldn't wait forever, that one day she would come for you—why did you go on with it all? Why did you ever pretend you loved me?

Her tears fell among the flowers she was arranging and lay like glistening dewdrops in the deep blood-red heart of the roses. And she stared at the beauty of the bouquet she was fashioning and thought how ironic it was that it should be a wedding bouquet, the symbol of love and hope and confidence in the future. When what she felt she ought to be making was a funeral wreath— to symbolise the death of her own lonely heart.

The afternoon came to an end at last, and Jenna locked the shop and drove slowly home. She was still trying to decide just what she would say to Dair when she came into the yard and saw his Range Rover parked in its usual spot.

So he had left Lysette's cottage. By now he would know that Jenna had been there. He would know that there was no further use in lying.

He was in the kitchen when Jenna came in, filling the kettle. There was a tray on the counter, set with two cups. He turned as she came in, and gave her the un-smiling glance that had become his normal greeting these days.

'I'm just making a cup of tea. Would you like one?' His tone was stiff and she felt a stab of pain at what they had lost. Followed swiftly by anger. Whose fault was it it had been lost, after all?

'So I see.' She took off her coat and took it through to the lobby to hang it up. 'You don't think something stronger might be more appropriate?'

'Sorry?' He looked puzzled, and Jenna had to restrain herself from hitting him. She gave him a contemptuous look.

'After your strenuous afternoon out on the moors. Don't you want something stronger than tea? Or maybe you've already had it? She seemed to have plenty of drinks on hand, from what I saw.'

His brows came together as he stared at her. 'Jenna, just what are you talking about? Where d'you think I've been?'

'I don't *think* you've been anywhere,' she said scathingly. 'I *know*. You've been out to Sampford Spiney, to see your mistress. I suppose that's where you've been going every time you've left the farm. Well, it's a cosy little love-nest right enough, but I don't know why you're bothering to be so secretive about it. *She* certainly doesn't seem to want to keep it quiet.' Her voice rose and trembled, and to her fury she felt the tears hot in her eyes.

Dair finished filling the kettle. He switched it on, his movements slow and deliberate as if he were thinking hard, and then he turned again to face her.

'Jenna, will you please calm down and tell me exactly what you mean by all this? What mistress am I supposed to be keeping out at Sampford Spiney? And just why do you think I've been there this afternoon?' His face was grim, his eyes like flints sparking with anger. 'Has someone been talking to you—making accusations without any foundation other than the occasional glimpse of me out checking sheep? Because that's all I've been doing out on the moors, I can assure you.'

Jenna stared at him, her anger rising swiftly to a peak. 'For goodness' sake, Dair—just how long are you going to keep this pretence up? You must know by now that it's no use. Or didn't she tell you I'd been there this morning?' Bitterness turned her voice to a whip. 'I suppose you had "better things to do". Or perhaps you both had a good laugh over it all. Well, I'm sorry, but the joke's over and it was never very funny anyway, as far as I was concerned. I'd just like to know what you mean to do about it.'

Dair took a step towards her, and she flinched involuntarily at the dark fury in his face. 'Just what are you saying, Jenna? *What in hell's name are you talking about?*'

'Don't pretend you don't know!' she flashed. 'Do you think I didn't see you this morning, on your way there? Do you really expect me to believe that she wouldn't have—wouldn't have told you how she scored over me?' Pain and humiliation brought fresh tears to her eyes, made her voice shake. Despising her own weakness, she hit out at him in the only way she knew. 'I'm beginning to believe you don't even know when you're lying, Dair Adams. I'm beginning to think you believe your own twisted fantasies.'

The kettle came to the boil and switched itself off. Neither of them noticed it. Jenna was staring at Dair, her breath coming quickly, and he was glowering back at her, his dark blue eyes smouldering with fury.

'I think you'd better explain just what you mean by that tirade,' he grated, and she shivered at the note of menace in his voice. 'Just where did you think you saw me this morning? And who is this "she" you keep talking about?' He came towards her, swift and silent as a panther, and gripped her arms so tightly that she cried out. 'And what the hell do you mean by talking about lies and fantasies?'

Jenna bit back her pain and met his eyes with a de-
fiance that hid her sudden fear. Dair was big, his strength
stemming from hard work and natural fitness, and she
had never before experienced this quivering fury that
transmitted itself through his fingers. Until now, she had
never feared him physically. But then she would never
have believed him to be a liar—and she'd been wrong
about that... Suddenly, she wished that the farm were
less isolated. A streetful of neighbours would have been
a welcome comfort just then.

'Well?' he growled. 'I'm waiting, Jenna.'

Jenna took a deep breath. What had she to lose after
all?

'All right. So you're still pretending. Well, let's see
what you have to say to this. I know you've been lying
to me, Dair! I *know* that Lysette isn't dead. Why not
be honest and tell me the truth, for goodness' sake, and
then I'll know what to do with the wreck you've made
of my life?'

'The wreck I've made of *your* life?' he repeated. 'And
what about the havoc you've created in mine? What
about the hopes *I* had—shattered before we even began
our honeymoon? Since you're so keen on honesty, Jenna,
why don't you try a little yourself? Tell me why you
turned against me the minute we'd cut the cake? Why
you put on such an act of being in love, wanting to marry
me—and then closed up against me the second it was
all signed and sealed?' His eyes narrowed and he shook
her by the arms, his fingers biting cruelly into her flesh.
'I've thought and thought about that, Jenna,' he ground
out, 'and all I can think is that it was to do with your
business. You'd got into deep water there, hadn't you—
rented expensive accommodation, bought a lot of
equipment? You wanted out, but you wanted to be sure

of something else to go to—and I filled the bill nicely.
I was even willing to help you start up a new business,
heaven help me!' His eyes were bitter and disillusioned
as he stared at her. 'I fell for it, the whole bit. Hook,
line and sinker. You really had me fooled. And maybe
it wouldn't have been so bad at that—if you'd been prepared to fulfil even a part of the bargain.'

Jenna's eyes were wide with shock. She couldn't believe the things she was hearing, the twisted, distorted
view of her that Dair had formed. How could he even
begin to think...?

'What bargain?' she whispered. 'I don't know what
you mean——'

'Don't you?' He laughed harshly. 'Well, maybe you
don't, at that. Maybe you really don't see what you
should be giving in return for it all. I'll spell it out for
you, shall I?' His mouth was grim, his eyes like stone,
a Dair Jenna had never seen before. 'So I was being
taken for a ride, used as a ticket out of London and into
a small town where you could queen it as lady of the
manor and set up your own twee little flower shop. But
surely even you expected to do *something* to earn it—
like behaving as a wife, just once in a while?'

'I think,' Jenna said coldly, 'that I've been quite
enough as a wife for you in the past few weeks.'

'Certainly, if I were the kind of husband who likes to
rape his wife every night,' Dair answered brutally. 'As
it happens, I'm not.' He looked at her and she saw con-
tempt in his eyes. 'You can have no conception of what
those nights did to me, Jenna,' he said quietly. 'I'd been
tormented beyond endurance—I didn't seem able to help
myself. I'd make love to you—if you can call it that—
in anger and frustration to begin with, and then the
tenderness, the love I still felt for you, would take over

and I'd forget the misery and the humiliation and give myself to you. Perhaps this time it will work, I'd think, perhaps this time I'll find the Jenna I loved. And for a while, it seemed that I did.' His eyes were dark, filled with pain. 'But come the morning, I'd know it was all a sham. A dream turned once again to nightmare. And to cap it all, you'd start asking about Lysette.' He dropped his hands from her arms and turned away, his fingers running through his hair. 'It's an obsession with you, and I don't know why.'

'You don't?' For a few moments, Jenna had begun to feel distress at the picture he painted. Had it really been like that for him? Had he been as unhappy as she, from a torment that was so much the same, yet stemmed from so different a cause? But his last words jerked her back to reality, reminding her too of his accusation—that she'd married him, basically, for money and a position. An accusation that was both unjust and untrue.

'You really don't know why I keep asking about Lysette—why I'm *obsessed* with her?' she asked slowly. 'Well, think about it, Dair. Think about it. Maybe it's because I don't much like being lied to—especially when I know you're lying. And I *do* know, Dair. Lysette isn't dead. She's very much alive. I've seen her and talked to her, so please don't bother to deny it any more. What's more, I believe her when she says you intend to divorce me and marry her. Yes, she told me that,' she added, seeing the astonishment flash into his eyes. 'She, at least, didn't try to pretend—why should she? And why should you, Dair? Why go on with it?'

He shook his head, and for a moment she thought she saw honest bewilderment in his eyes. Honest bewilderment, indeed—it just proved what a good actor he was! And how easily taken in she still could be, if she wasn't on her guard.

'Well?' she asked icily. 'What are you going to say to that?'

He shook his head again.

'What can I say? You seem to have it all worked out. As far as I can see, there are only two possibilities—either you're the one who's having fantasies, or you've met someone who——' He stopped suddenly and his brows came down over his eyes. He gave her a sudden, sharp glance and then went on more slowly '—you've met someone who's convinced you that she's Lysette.'

'And who do you suppose that could be?' Jenna asked sarcastically. 'Did Lysette have a double? Someone exactly like her, who also wanted to marry you? Do you really expect me to believe that, Dair? Because I shan't, you know.'

He looked at her for a long moment, then lifted his shoulders in a shrug, turning away with an expression of resignation.

'There's not a lot of point in saying it, then, is there?' He walked to the window and looked out into the darkness. 'And that just about sums up our relationship, doesn't it, Jenna? A stalemate of non-belief on both sides.'

'Yes,' she said hopelessly, 'I suppose it does.'

'So...' He turned and walked back to her, standing just within arm's reach but without touching her, his eyes looking gravely down into hers, dark and unreadable. 'Where do we go from here? Do we call it a day?'

Jenna swallowed. Now that they had come to this point, she wanted desperately to draw back, to wipe out the last half-hour, to go on—yes, if necessary to go on living a lie. Just so that she could be with Dair, sharing the same house, the same life. Because nothing that had happened had managed to kill her love. It was still there, smouldering inside her, the brightness of its flame dimmed but its heat as intense as ever.

'Is that what you want?' she asked at last, her words coming in a husky whisper from a throat that was dry and painful.

He stared at her, and she saw the deep unhappiness in his eyes, the pain and bewilderment that she had seen before and disbelieved. Could he really be so good an actor? And if so, why should he want to deceive her? He must know she had seen Lysette—why go on trying to deny the truth?

'No,' he said at last, and his voice was as ragged as her own. 'It isn't what I want, Jenna. What I want is a normal, happy marriage with you. What I want is your love, given honestly and freely as I thought you gave it before we were married.' He paused. 'I don't even want to know why it all changed,' he said in a low voice. 'Just so long as we can be as we were then.'

Jenna looked up at him. He had spoken so simply, his voice tired and hopeless—and, she could have sworn, utterly sincere. And her eyes filled with tears.

She stretched out her hands towards him.

'Don't you think it's what I want too?' she asked shakily. 'Don't you think I've longed for those days, when we were so happy? Oh, Dair—I've missed you so much. It's been like living with a shadow.'

Her voice trembled and shook into silence, and with the last words the tears came. She stood before him and sobbed without restraint, her defences broken down at last. And when she felt his arms come round her to draw her close against him, she didn't try to resist. She wept against his broad chest, feeling his heart beneath her cheek and knowing that they had come at last to their crossroads and would have to choose which way to take.

'Jenna,' he said at last, 'I don't know what to say.'

'Just tell me the truth,' she whispered painfully. 'I can't bear any more lies, Dair.'

There was a long silence. She looked up at last, her tears coming more slowly now, and saw his face set like a stone. Her heart sank. What was it that brought that grimness to his eyes? Did he, even now, mean to go on hiding the truth? Or was he about to tell her that their marriage was indeed at an end?

But when he spoke, Dair's voice was oddly gentle. 'Come and sit down, Jenna,' he said quietly. 'Let me make that tea. And then I'll tell you everything.' He hesitated, and then added, 'Everything I know, that is.'

Everything he knew? Jenna allowed him to lead her into the sitting-room, her head spinning. What did he mean by that? Surely he must know the whole story of something that concerned him so deeply. Surely he must know that what he'd been telling her just wasn't true.

Her suspicions returned, and along with them a new fear. She'd flung at him the accusation that he didn't even know what truth was, that he didn't know when he was lying. She hadn't meant it, of course—but could that be an explanation? Was there something in Dair, some aberration that really *didn't* recognise the truth?

It was the most frightening thought she'd had yet.

As tenderly as if she were made of precious porcelain, Dair set her on the couch and then went to make the tea. Jenna sat silent, trying not to let her mind play with these new and horrifying ideas. When he returned with the tray, she looked up at him doubtfully. He met her eyes with a gravity she could have sworn was sincere, and began to pour out the tea. Then he settled himself in an armchair close to her couch, where they could see each other.

'What shall I tell you first, Jenna?' he asked, and she shook her head unbelievingly.

'Why—everything, Dair. About Lysette. Why you told me she was dead. Why you've kept on telling me that, even though you knew I had to find out the truth eventually. Why you didn't marry her—and why you married me.' Her voice choked on the last words, his face was misted through her tears, but she refused to look away. 'Why did you do it, Dair?' she whispered. 'Why did you marry me—knowing that you loved her all the time?'

Dair sighed. He picked up his cup and sipped it, an automatic gesture. He set it down again, shaking his head, and his eyes were direct as he met her anguished gaze.

'Jenna, it wasn't like that. You must believe me, it was never like that. Lysette and I—it was all over before I met you. There was no possibility of it ever starting again. Before I tell you anything else, you've got to believe that.'

'How can I?' she cried. 'When I saw you kissing her photograph on the very day we were married—before we set off on our honeymoon! How *can* I believe it was over?'

He stared at her, his frown vague as if he were trying to remember, and then his expression cleared and horror widened his eyes.

'You saw that? My darling, why didn't you say so? Why didn't you ask me then?'

'I couldn't. Aunt Mickie told me never to ask you about Lysette. She said you'd tell me in your own time—

but you never did, did you?' Jenna gazed at him hope-lessly. 'And when I did ask you, you lied to me.'

'No, Jenna,' he said quietly. 'I never lied to you. All right, I never told you the truth either, and I see now that I was wrong. But there are things you don't know, things you don't understand. It wasn't so easy...' He stopped, as if searching for words, and Jenna saw that his eyes were shadowed, as if filled with their own pain. She waited, still bewildered. What was he saying?

'Tell me,' she said simply, but it was several moments before he spoke again, and when he did she thought he was going to refuse her once more.

'It still isn't easy.' He stopped again, then seemed to make up his mind and reached out towards her, his hand palm upwards. 'Jenna, you have to trust me. You've got to believe me—when I tell you again that Lysette is dead, when I——'

'*No!*' Her disappointment almost too much to bear, Jenna struck at his hand, pushing it violently away. 'Dair, how can you? You talk about trust and then in the next breath you tell me the same old lie. I tell you, I *know* the truth. Lysette *isn't* dead. I told you, I've seen her and talked to her. I delivered flowers to her today, in that cottage at Sampford Spiney. Why do you keep per-sisting in this? What possible good can it do you now?' She leapt to her feet, scarcely knowing what she was doing as her fury took full possession of her. 'You've done this to me so many times!' she cried. 'You lead me on, you make me think you love me, you ask for my trust—and then out they come again, the same old lies! Just how much do you think I can take, Dair? Just how stupid do you think I am? Oh——' unable to tolerate any more, she whipped away from him '—it's just no use even trying to talk to you. You really *don't* know the difference between truth and lies. You're sick, Dair, that's what it is—sick. Well, you can stay by yourself and make up your fantasies if it pleases you, or you can go to *her*, and good luck to you both. I've had as much as I can take!'

As Dair came to his feet and reached out for her, she thrust past him and fled from the room. She felt her leg knock against the coffee-table, heard the crash as the tea-tray fell to the floor, heard Dair's voice calling her name, but she was beyond reason now, beyond any kind of response. Her heart thudding in her throat, the tears pouring down her cheeks, she ran up the stairs, into her room and slammed and locked the door behind her.

Dair came once to the door, calling her name, pleading with her to come out and listen to him. Then he too grew angry; she heard him go down the stairs again and although she wanted to call him back, she lay silent, her head buried in her pillow. She could take no more; she wanted only to sleep, to forget all the pain and misery, to bury her unhappiness in her dreams.

But sleep would not come. And Jenna lay awake throughout the night, staring blindly into the darkness until, slowly, it began to grow light and the sounds from the yard below told her that another day had begun on the farm. That Dair had left the house and gone out to start his daily work, leaving her alone.

Slowly, heavily, Jenna dragged herself to the window and stared down. She saw his Range Rover leave the yard and drive along the moorland road, and she knew without doubt that he was going to Lysette.

CHAPTER EIGHT

A STRANGE tremor passed over Jenna as she stared down into the yard and thought of what had happened on the previous evening.

The quarrel and its bitter aftermath had left her with a throbbing head and a sickness that seemed to come from her stomach and spread weariness through her whole body. She felt empty, but the thought of food nauseated her and when she went down to the kitchen and made herself some coffee, she couldn't drink it.

As she slowly prepared to go to the shop, she was haunted by the feeling that she and Dair had stood together at a crossroads and taken the wrong path... For a short time, it had seemed that there was still real feeling between them, the kind of love that could surmount any obstacle.

And then it had been swept away again, destroyed—surely forever—by Dair's continued insistence that Lysette was dead.

Why did he persist in this lie? What could he possibly hope to achieve by it? She was unable to stop the problem circling in her head. She supposed he must have some reason and that eventually it would be revealed to her—presumably when he faced her at last with Lysette and told her that their marriage was over and that he intended to make the glamorous blonde his wife, as she should have been all along.

That, Jenna was convinced, was the only logical outcome of this nightmare—though why Dair was postponing it, she couldn't begin to think.

And that brought her back, full circle, to the original problem. No wonder her head spun; no wonder she felt ill and weak, and as if she wanted to do nothing but crawl into bed and find the sleep that had eluded her all night.

Perhaps she should ring the shop, tell Cindy she wasn't well and wouldn't be in today. But the thought of staying in the house, while Dair went to see his mistress, was even worse. It would be better to get out, to immerse herself in work, listening to Cindy's cheerful chatter and making herself smile at the customers.

Cindy, however, took a different view.

'My stars!' she exclaimed when Jenna arrived at the shop. 'You look proper washed out—are you feeling all right? Not got flu, have you?'

'I don't think so. Just a bit tired. What have we got on this morning?' Jenna brushed aside Cindy's concern and looked at the order book. 'We'd better concentrate on making Christmas wreaths, I think—we're going to have quite a demand for them, by the look of it.'

'Yes, that's what I thought. I've made a start. Jenna, are you sure you should have come in? You look really pale.'

'I'm all right.' Jenna saw Cindy flinch at the sharpness of her voice, and flushed. 'I'm sorry, Cindy, I didn't mean to speak like that. I do feel a bit off colour this morning, but I'm sure it'll wear off. To tell you the truth, I haven't felt really well since that tummy bug a few weeks ago.'

It wasn't strictly true, but she had been extra tired during the past few days and if she thought she knew her weariness was caused more by the state of her marriage than by any bug, she wasn't prepared to tell Cindy that. Confiding in anyone else would be an admission of failure—and Jenna wasn't ready for that even now.

'Well, I think you ought to see a doctor if it doesn't get any better. Bugs like that only last a few days as a rule.' Cindy went through to the back of the shop, where she had been busy making Christmas wreaths with a pile of holly that had been delivered the previous day. 'Look, what do you think of this?'

'It's lovely.' Thankful to have attention diverted from herself, Jenna took the completed wreath in her hands and admired it. Cindy had woven Christmas roses and fir cones in with the shining holly and packed it all well with moss so that it would last. 'We'll put this one in the window as our showpiece. You really are clever at this kind of thing, Cindy.'

'Well, I enjoy it.' The younger girl took the wreath back and gazed at it critically. 'Hmm, not bad...' There was a pensiveness in her eyes and she glanced up at Jenna, her expression suddenly shy. 'Jenna...'

'Mm? What is it?'

'Something I wanted to ask you.' For once, Cindy seemed to have difficulty in finding words, and Jenna looked at her with surprise.

'A problem? Is it Tanya?'

'No, Tanya's fine. Well—at least, it *is* to do with her in a way. In fact—it's almost all to do with her, I suppose.' Cindy caught Jenna's eye and laughed. 'I'm not making much sense, am I? As a matter of fact—it's me and Rob.'

'Oh.' Jenna sat down and looked at her assistant. She felt guilty that she hadn't seen this coming—she'd known Cindy and Rob were friendly, but nothing had been said for some time and the matter had slipped out of her mind.

And she hadn't even seen much of Rob lately. She racked her brains to try to remember when she had last visited him at the cottage. Not since that day when she'd told him about herself and Dair. She felt ashamed, as if she'd just been using him.

But it wasn't the moment to think about herself now. Cindy was looking at her with anxious eyes, evidently wanting to confide in her, and Jenna felt a fresh remorse, that she hadn't given the other girl her own confidences.

'Have you been seeing a lot of Rob?' she asked gently.

Cindy nodded. 'Quite a lot. It started that day I took Tanya out to his cottage to see Gypsy—the pup. Well, of course, once wasn't enough and Rob and I got on well and it was nice, going out there, playing with the dog on the moor, going for walks and having tea by the fire. I generally take something with me—crumpets to toast or some pasties I've made, some scones and cream, that sort of thing. And then we have a game of something—you know, the sort of thing Tanya can play, snakes and ladders and such—and then I bring her home. It's not been anything much—just friendly, you know.'

'It sounds lovely,' Jenna said, thinking wistfully of the evenings she and Dair had been spending by their own fireside, strained and unable to talk before Dair finally left her to go into the farm office. 'And now...?'

'Well—it's got a bit more than that now. We've been going out there all day Sundays. Or going for drives. Or Rob's come to our house.' Cindy looked down at the wreath on her lap. 'It's got so we don't like being apart any more,' she said in a low voice.

'But that's wonderful!' Jenna exclaimed. 'You and Rob—you're just right for each other. What's the problem?' She remembered what Cindy had said a few moments earlier. 'Doesn't Tanya get on with him?'

'Tanya loves him,' Cindy said simply. 'And that's just it.'

'How do you mean?'

'Well—you know how I'm placed. Tanya's never had a daddy. And with Chris dying the way he did—well, I never felt much like finding another man. I didn't think I'd ever want anyone else, you see. I used to blame myself—tell myself I ought to find someone, for her sake. So she'd know what a real family was like. But nobody ever came along that I could fancy.'

'Until Rob,' Jenna said softly.

'That's right. And we just seemed to click straight away. It was as if we'd always known each other. I know it sounds corny, but it really was like that.'

Cindy fell silent and Jenna gazed at her almost with envy. It seemed so simple, the way Cindy described it. As if they'd always known each other. But hadn't it been like that once for herself and Dair? And hadn't it changed, brutally, painfully?

'So what *is* the problem?' she asked. 'Does Rob—does he feel the same?'

'Oh, yes. He says he does. And—and I know he does. He's asked me to marry him, Jenna.' There was real joy in Cindy's eyes, but it was mingled with doubt. 'The only thing is—am I being fair to him if I do? I mean, how do I know I'm not doing it just to give Tanya a daddy? You see, when she was first born I was really bitter about losing Chris. I used to think it was worse for her than for me. She'd never known him. And it just didn't seem fair—that tiny baby, losing her father before she was even born. I used to think I'd do anything, *any-thing*, to bring him back for her.' She paused and then asked piteously, 'How do I know I'm not doing that now? Marrying Rob because he'll be a father to her? A substitute for Chris. Because if I am—well, it's wrong, isn't it? It's not fair to either of them.'

'No, it wouldn't be—if that *were* what you're doing.' Jenna looked at Cindy thoughtfully. 'But I don't think it is, is it? You honestly love him, and surely that's all that matters. If Tanya ends up with a father she can love—well, that's all the better. But I don't believe it's your main reason.'

'I wish I knew,' Cindy said hopelessly. 'But I've thought about it so much, I honestly don't know what I do think any more. All I know is—it's no fun, being a single parent. I sometimes think I'd do anything to have someone to share it with. And I'm afraid that's what's happening now.'

Jenna shook her head. 'I don't believe it. I've seen you when Rob's come into the shop. You light up, Cindy—and so does he. Look—it's got to be your decision, and I'm the last person to give you advice. But if it were me—I'd stop worrying. Let it all be as simple as I believe it is. Rob and you love each other, and you both love Tanya. What more can you ask?'

The shop bell rang and Cindy got up and hurried through. Jenna sat still, gazing at the wreath, at the pile of holly, at the flowers that stood in buckets of water waiting to be arranged into bouquets or bought loose. She thought over the past half-hour and her lips twisted ruefully.

If only Cindy knew just what a mess her own life was in, she would never have asked Jenna's advice!

*   *   *

Gradually, as the day wore on, Jenna began to feel better, and by the time Cindy left at lunchtime she was able to pin on a smile and say that she felt fine, Cindy was to go home as usual and not worry. 'I just had a bad night,' she said. 'I'm OK now, really.'

'Well, if you're sure...' Cindy looked her over critically. 'I must say, you do have more colour now, but you still look strained to me. Are you sure everything's all right, Jenna?'

'Quite sure.' Firmly, Jenna pushed her towards the door. 'Now, if you'll just do that one delivery to the nursing home... I don't expect we'll be busy this afternoon. I'll make some more wreaths. I think we're going to do well with those.'

'Yes, we've had some orders already. All right, Jenna, I'll see you tomorrow. But don't do too much—you really do look tired.'

'I told you, I had a bad night. Now, stop treating me like Tanya and go home!' Jenna watched her assistant go and then returned to the back room, wondering why she hadn't confided in Cindy. The two had become friends as they'd worked together, and Cindy had been willing to confide her own worries; she would have been a ready and sympathetic listener to Jenna.

But how could she possibly have understood? With all her troubles, Cindy had never faced the kind of problems that beset Jenna. She had been genuinely loved by the men in her life—Chris, so tragically killed, and now Rob. She had never known what it was to be lied to, deceived.

The words brought a shudder to Jenna's heart. Even now, it seemed incredible that they could be applied to Dair. Yet what else could she possibly believe?

She ate a quick lunch of yoghurt and a banana, and set to work on the wreaths Cindy had started. They were making three different styles and Jenna decided to make one each of the two that Cindy had not yet done, so that all three could be displayed in the window. She sat working at the holly, weaving it in and out of the wire, her mind still circling around the unhappiness it could not forget.

The sound of the shop bell brought her to her feet. But before she could reach the door to the shop, it was thrust violently open and she jumped back, startled.

'*Dair!* What are you doing here?' Briefly, painfully, she remembered that other time when he had come un-expectedly to the shop—on Goose Fair day, when it had seemed for a while that everything was going to be all right . . . when she had seen Lysette for the first time. 'What do you want?' she asked, retreating before the grim look on his face.

'I want you to shut the shop and come with me. No——' he raised his hand against her immediate protest '—don't bother to say anything. It won't hurt Tavistock if it can't buy any flowers for one day. And you can leave what you're doing. But I'm taking you out of here, Jenna, now, and if you make it necessary I'll do it by force. Don't make any mistake about that.'

Jenna looked at him and knew he meant it. His face was set like granite, his eyes as hard as iron. There was a simmering determination about him that brought a shiver of apprehension to her heart. Where did he mean to take her? What did he mean to do?

'Dair——' she began, but again he stopped her.

'I've told you, I'll brook no argument, Jenna. Either you put your coat on now and come willingly, or I pick you up and carry you out into the street, kicking and screaming if that's how you want it. Now—which is it to be?' He moved a little closer. 'I warn you, Jenna— I've had just about as much as I can take from you. I don't have an unlimited stock of patience.'

He reached out, unhooked Jenna's jacket from the wall and held it out. Slowly, unwillingly, she reached out to take it from him, but he shook his head and held it for her to slip her arms into.

'Never let it be said that I forgot my manners.'

His voice was ironic and Jenna flung him a glance of pure dislike as she turned her back on him to allow him to slide the jacket up her arms. As he did so, she felt his hands brush against her, and a tingle ran through her body. Even now, she thought, cursing her own weakness—even after all that's happened—oh, why couldn't she be free of him, *why*?

'Where are we going?' she asked as he gripped her shoulder and led her out of the shop. 'How long will we be?'

'You'll see. Just put the "Closed" sign up and lock the door. The Range Rover's right outside.' As they came out of the shop, two women passed and Jenna recognised them as customers. They smiled at Jenna and one of them made a remark about how nice it was to see Mrs Adams going out for lunch with her husband. They disappeared down the street and Jenna stared after them with an impotent mixture of anger and despair.

'You realise you're kidnapping me?' she said, and realised at once how ludicrous this sounded. But Dair didn't seem to be amused. He opened the car door and thrust her inside.

'If those are the lengths I have to go to to make you see sense, yes,' he said as he climbed in the other side.

'I'm quite sure you'd never have agreed to come voluntarily.'

'That depends on where we're going, doesn't it?' She stared out as Dair pulled away from the kerb and headed out of town. 'Dair, what's all this about?'

'You tell me.' They were on the Whitchurch road now. 'I don't even know where we're heading for myself—except that it's Sampford Spiney. You'll have to tell me where the cottage is.'

'The cot——?' Jenna stared at him. '*Sampford Spiney?* Dair—you're not taking me to—to——'

'To visit this mythical mistress of mine, yes.' He turned up past the little church with its square tower and the inn at its gates. 'Then maybe we'll find out the truth of all this. Don't you think that's a good idea?'

Jenna opened her mouth and then closed it again. Her thoughts were too incoherent to express. She shook her head violently in an effort to clear it, then tried again.

'Let's get this straight.' Her voice quivered. 'You're taking me to Sampford Spiney—to Lysette's cottage?'

'To where you delivered the flowers,' he corrected her. 'Where you say you thought you saw Lysette, yes.'

'What do you mean, where I *say I thought I saw her*?' Jenna flared. 'I *did* see her! I told you—I talked to her, she told me everything—how you and she were going to get married as soon as you'd divorced me, how you knew from the beginning that our marriage had been a mistake but your *sense of honour*—and that's a laugh!—had made you try to make a success of it. Well, you didn't try very hard, that's all I can say. There's more to a successful marriage than sex, Dair—and even that was a pretty dismal failure, wasn't it?'

Dair pulled the Range Rover in to the side of the road and slammed on the brakes. He unbuckled his seatbelt and turned to Jenna, his hands on her shoulders. His face was livid with anger.

'No, it wasn't,' he snarled. 'It wasn't a failure at all, and you know it. You enjoyed those encounters as much as I did, Jenna—oh, yes, you may have protested to begin with, but you soon settled down to get as much pleasure out of them as you gave me. Yes, pleasure.' His voice was caustic. 'Pleasure and happiness—even if it didn't last.' He threw her a look that seared her to her soul. 'You don't have to tell me sex isn't everything,' he said scathingly. 'We've proved it.'

Jenna sat silent. His words were like a knife twisting in her heart. She thought of the nights when they had lain together, the anger that their lovemaking had driven away only to return when the ecstasy had passed and the world had begun to intrude again. When reality had reared its ugly head.

'It's a pity you didn't keep away from me, then, if that's how you feel,' she said, and wished at once that she had not spoken. There was so much bitterness in her voice, such deep unhappiness. 'In fact, it's a pity we ever met.'

Dair looked at her for a long moment. Then he released her shoulders and turned away, looking out across the moor to the distant tors. His face was averted so that she could not see his expression, but when he spoke there was a note in his voice that she recognised, a note of pain that equated with her own and brought anguish to her heart.

'I wish I could agree with you there, Jenna. But even after all that's happened . . . I still believe there's something for us. If we can only get this mess sorted out, find out the truth of what's been happening . . .' He sighed, almost as if he felt himself already defeated, and then turned back to her. 'Jenna, let's make a bargain. If we can resolve this today, and we can put it all behind us and begin again, let's try. Let's give ourselves another chance. If we can't—well, we'll part, with as few hard feelings as we can. Admit we've made a mistake somewhere along the line, and go our own ways.' His eyes met hers. 'And I tell you now, I hope it won't come to that. I *believe* it won't come to that. What do you say?'

Jenna searched his face. What was he doing, bringing her out here? What motive could he possibly have in facing her with his mistress, while still insisting that such a person didn't exist? She thought again of her suspicion that there was something wrong with him, that he didn't even know when he was lying, but as she looked into the sapphire eyes, dark with urgency, her whole being cried out against such an idea. Dair was as sane and whole as she was herself—of that, she was convinced.

Perhaps it's really me that's going mad, she thought confusedly. Perhaps I never did see Lysette—perhaps I imagined and dreamed the whole thing.

'Well, Jenna?' Dair's voice was gentle, as gentle as it had ever been during their short engagement or when he had made love to her in the big bedroom at the farm. 'What do you say? One more chance?'

What could she say? Whatever happened this afternoon, she knew it had to be decisive. She met his eyes and nodded slowly.

'One more chance, Dair.' But her heart told her the chance was slight—so slight as to be almost non-existent. She *had* seen Lysette. It hadn't been a dream. And nothing could change the truth.

Dair started up the Range Rover again and drove silently across the moor. Already, the afternoon was

growing dark; a bank of bruised clouds lowered threat-
eningly in the sky and the tors were stark and grey against
the horizon. The village of Sampford Spiney, as they
approached it, seemed to be cringing into the hillside as
if afraid of impending storm.

'You'll have to tell me which cottage it is,' Dair said
quietly as they came to the first huddle of houses, and
Jenna turned her head to stare at him.

'But you *know*——'

'Jenna—please. We agreed on one more chance. Now,
whatever you believe, I tell you I *don't* know which
cottage this—this woman lives in.' He sighed. 'All right.
Let's put it another way. Which cottage did you deliver
the flowers to?'

'Over there.' She pointed. 'At the end of that track.'

'I see.' He looked doubtfully at the narrow, overgrown drive. 'I think I'd better park here. Is it far along
the track?'

'Only a few yards,' Jenna said stiffly. He *knew*—how
could he possibly maintain the fiction that he'd never
been here before?

Dair stopped the Range Rover and jumped down.
Jenna followed him slowly and they stood for a moment
at the end of the track, looking along it to where the
cottage could now be seen half hidden behind the straggling bushes.

'So this is my love-nest, is it?' he murmured, and held
out his hand. 'Come along, Jenna. Whoever lives here,
we're going to face them together.'

More bewildered than ever, Jenna let him draw her
along the track. His hand was warm around hers, strong
and reassuring. The conflict between the facts as she
knew them and the version Dair had insisted was the
truth, a conflict that appeared impossible to resolve,

brought a fresh sickness to her stomach, an apprehension that was very nearly intolerable. She wanted to see what would happen when they reached the door, when Lysette opened it and faced them at last; equally, she wanted to pull her hand out of Dair's and run away.

As if he sensed her disturbed thoughts, he tightened his fingers around hers and turned his head to look down at her. He didn't smile, but the warmth in his glance seemed to bring a glow to the chill of her heart and she felt a sudden conviction that everything was going to be all right. There *was* going to be some explanation to all this. She and Dair were going to have their second chance.

The cottage looked dark, its windows like blind eyes staring across the bleak loneliness of the moor. Lysette must be in the room at the back, the tiny kitchen behind the main room.

They stopped in front of the door. Dair looked at it, at the darkened windows, the clinging undergrowth of the neglected garden.

'It doesn't look as if anyone's lived here for months,' he said.

Jenna turned her eyes towards him and the brief warmth receded, leaving her heart even colder than before.

'Please,' she said in a low, aching voice. 'Please, Dair...'

He glanced at her and then raised his hand to knock on the door. And in that moment, Jenna knew the truth.

'Nobody at home,' he remarked as if they had called in to pay an unexpected social visit.

'*Please.*'

The door had an old-fashioned handle with a large keyhole. It was almost certainly locked. But when she reached out and touched it, it gave under Jenna's hand. She pushed and the door swung back. She threw a quick look at Dair, and then walked in.

There was nobody there. And in the rapidly growing darkness, she knew that nobody was coming back to it. Not Lysette; not anybody. The cottage was empty.

The furniture was still in place—the old-fashioned armchairs, the rugs, the flowered curtains, the side table on which Lysette had set out elegant wine glasses. But the glasses and the bottles were no longer there. The bone-china cups had vanished. The pretty cushions had gone.

If Lysette had ever been here, she no longer was. She had flown—like the bird of paradise, the beautiful butterfly she so much resembled. And standing there in the cottage, its cold seeping into her bones as the first snowflakes began to fall outside, Jenna thought that at last she understood.

She turned to Dair, and her eyes were blazing. But before she could open her mouth, he began to speak.

'There you are, Jenna. There's nobody here—nobody at all. There never has been.' He moved closer, as if about to take her in his arms. 'It was all imagination, don't you see?' he murmured. 'You've let this obsession run away with you, Jenna. All right, so you brought some flowers here—perhaps you even saw someone, a cleaner or neighbour, someone like that. And then you—well——'

'Imagined everything!' she flashed at him. 'Oh, yes, Dair—very neat. Very clever! But not quite clever enough—because I *know* what happened, who I saw and talked to and what she said. And nothing you do or say will ever convince me otherwise.' She stepped away from him, holding out her hands to ward him off. 'If you're trying, for some reason best known to yourself, to persuade me that I'm going mad,' she said painfully, 'you've failed. And this—this charade of bringing me here, pretending you didn't know where you were coming, when you knew all the time that she'd be gone—well, it just won't work. What kind of a fool do you take me for, Dair? And why *bother*? Why not just *tell* me you want a divorce? Why go all around the mountain to get there?'

Dair lifted both hands. 'Because I don't *want* one! Can't you understand that? I want our marriage to succeed, Jenna. That's all I've ever wanted.' He ran his hand through his hair. 'Look, I don't know what the hell's been going on here, but you can see there was never anyone here. And whoever it was, it couldn't have been Lysette. Because Lysette's——'

'Dead,' Jenna finished for him. 'All right, Dair. So she's dead. So I've been seeing ghosts. Talking to a ghost—delivering flowers to a ghost. All right—if you insist on having it that way, you have it that way. Stay here with your ghost. And I wish you well of her.'

She walked past him, out into the bitter wind. It was almost fully dark now and the snow had begun in earnest. Thick white flakes whirled down into her face, touching her skin with soft, ice-cold fingers. But Jenna was barely aware of them, or of the tears that streamed from her eyes to freeze against her cheeks. Blindly, ignoring Dair's voice as he followed her from the cottage, she stumbled down the rutted track and walked out into the road, past the Range Rover and on to the moor.

'Jenna! Come back! You can't go off alone—it's dark, it's snowing, it's dangerous.' His voice was filled with anxiety, with something that she would once have called love and now could think of only as deceit. 'Jenna, come back...'

But Jenna did not turn her head. Her [...]
apart with the pain of this final betrayal, she w[...]
What did she care for the danger of straying acros[...]
moor, treacherous enough at its best and deadly on a
cold December night with snow falling? What did she
care for anything?

Nothing that happened now could be any worse than
what Dair had done to her.

CHAPTER NINE

HE CAUGHT up with her almost at once.

'Jenna! What the hell do you think you're doing, rushing off like that?' His hands were rough as they grasped her by the shoulders and spun her round to face him. 'Have you gone mad? You know what Dartmoor's like—it must be the coldest night of the year, and it's snowing. What's got into you?' He pulled her against him, and for a moment Jenna was tempted to rest against him, to let his warmth and strength envelop her. But almost as soon as she recognised it, she jerked herself away.

'Let me go! Leave me alone! Don't you *dare* to touch me!' Instantly, his fingers gripped her wrist in a hold she could not break; fruitlessly she tugged and twisted but, as if he didn't even notice her struggles, Dair turned and pulled her behind him, back to where the Range Rover waited. Reaching it, he tugged open the door and thrust her inside.

'And don't try to get out—I'll only catch you again.' He stamped around to climb in the driver's door and Jenna, realising that he did not intend to let her go, sat shivering in her seat. Staring straight ahead, she was conscious of his head turning to look at her; she bit her lip and refused silently to look back.

'Fasten your seatbelt,' he ordered her curtly, and started the engine. 'We're going home. We'll talk this out there.'

'There's nothing to talk about.'

'I happen to disagree.' He swung the Range Rover out of the village and trod hard on the accelerator. The powerful headlights lit up the narrow road, searing through the dancing snowflakes.

'Tough!' Jenna snapped. 'Because I'm not discussing this any more, Dair. I told you before, I've had enough. I don't know what you expected to achieve by that little farce, but whatever it was you failed. Miserably.'

'Look, I told you I knew nothing about the cottage, or whoever was living there. I'd have thought that what we've just seen would be enough to convince you. Jenna, I was as surprised as you to find it empty—after what you'd told me, I thought there must be someone there, someone playing tricks. Not very funny tricks, I'll agree, but maybe they weren't meant to be. But now—well, you've got to admit the place is empty. So who's trying to fool whom? Tell me that.'

'Well, it isn't me!' Jenna flashed. 'And I don't intend to discuss it any more. So will you please take me home— I've got some packing to do!'

There was a moment of stillness in the darkened car. Then Dair said quietly, 'Packing?'

'You don't imagine,' Jenna said coldly, 'that I intend to stay with you after this?'

As soon as the Range Rover halted in the yard, Jenna pulled open the door and scrambled out. The snow was already whitening the ground and a rising wind whipped it into tiny, fierce spicules that stung her cheeks. She ran across to the kitchen door and unlocked it.

Inside, it was warm and there was an appetising smell from the casserole Mrs Endicott had left simmering in the oven. Jenna snapped on the light and stood quite still for a moment, looking around. There was a homeliness here that caught at her heart. It was as if the house were speaking to her, saying 'Welcome home'—and she wanted, so badly, to feel that it was her home, that she was welcome here. But although her heart longed to tell her she was right to feel that, her reason told her she was wrong. And on the heels of her pain and bitterness came a great, overwhelming sadness.

Dair came into the kitchen behind her. He closed the door quietly and they looked at each other.

'You really mean this?' he asked. 'You really mean to go?'

'I have to. I can't stay here any longer. You must see that, Dair.'

He bowed his head. 'Jenna, I don't know what I see any more. I only know that everything's falling apart around me and I don't understand why. I can't believe that——' The shrilling of the telephone broke in on his words. He looked at her and lifted his hands helplessly.

'Go and answer it,' Jenna said tonelessly. 'It can't make any difference, Dair. Nothing can make any difference now.'

Without waiting for his reply, she turned and went out into the hall and up the stairs. Moving like a robot, she walked into the small room where they stored boxes and suitcases. She found her two largest cases and took them back into the bedroom.

It was difficult to know where to start. She wanted to take everything—but what *was* everything? Her clothes, of course—but there was so much more than clothes. Her whole life was here, the life she had taken to London, gathered around her in the flat, brought here to Devon. The life she had begun to make with Dair.

How did you pack away a life? How did you pack hopes and dreams, and shattered illusions?

Jenna opened the wardrobe and began aimlessly shuffling dresses on their hangers. She took out a skirt, considered it and put it back. How could she pack when she didn't even know where she was going?

The thought of going home, facing the questions her parents might not ask but would be unable to keep from their eyes, brought fresh tears to her eyes.

Denise? She supposed her friend would take her in. But Denise's last letter had mentioned a new man—and Jenna had a strong suspicion that by now he might have moved in with her. They wouldn't want Jenna descending on them.

Rob. Could she go to Rob?

As Jenna stood hesitating, she heard Dair's footsteps coming up the stairs. Hastily, she grabbed a few garments at random and threw them on the bed. But when Dair came in, he barely glanced at them.

'Jenna...'

'Please. Dair. Don't let's start again. I can't take any more, I just want to get away, I need to think——'

'Jenna, listen.' He reached out to her, an oddly diffident gesture, and then let his hand drop. 'It's all right, I'm not going to try to persuade you to stay—not for my sake, anyway.' Startled, she looked at him and saw that his face was taut with anxiety. Not angry, baffled or frustrated—just anxious. 'That phone call,' he said, 'it was from New Zealand.'

'New Zealand!' For a moment, it seemed too ludicrous to be real. What could a phone call from New Zealand have to do with all this, with the chaos their life had become?

Then she remembered. 'Aunt Mickie! Dair, what's wrong? Has something happened——'

'She's on her way home, Jenna. The call was from her friends there. Apparently, she's been ill—I don't know what's the matter, but her symptoms must have been pretty alarming because she was advised to come home as soon as possible. She caught a flight yesterday and she'll be at Heathrow early tomorrow morning.' He rubbed his hand over his face. 'Jenna, I'll have to go and fetch her. I'm bringing her here.'

He looked at her, and Jenna knew what he was asking. Slowly, she laid down the dress she was holding. She met his eyes and nodded slightly.

'You want me to stay. For Aunt Mickie's sake.'

'Lord knows,' he said with a wretched note in his voice, 'I want you to stay for mine. But I know it's no use asking that. Yes—I'm asking you to stay for her. Because I don't know just how ill she is, or even what the trouble is. All I know is there'll be doctors to see, hospital visits to arrange. And I know that if she comes home and finds we've broken up—well, it could kill her, Jenna.'

He said the words simply, but they fell like stones into the quiet room. And Jenna knew he was right. Mickie had taken the place of his mother, she loved Dair as a son. To come home and find his marriage in splinters would break her heart. And if she were seriously ill— yes, it could be the final blow.

She thought of Mickie's kindness to her. The way she'd welcomed her on that first visit. The warmth and love she'd always extended. The talks they'd had. And she knew she could not leave now.

She looked at the bed, at the clothes she had flung down on it. The suitcase. The symbols of a broken marriage . . . a broken heart.

It wasn't a chance to start again. She didn't believe they'd ever have that now. But it might be a reprieve.

'All right, Dair,' she said quietly. 'I'll stay.'

Dair arrived back with Aunt Mickie late the following afternoon, after a difficult journey on roads which were treacherous with snow. Jenna, telephoning Cindy first thing in the morning, had taken the day off from the shop and prepared the best of the spare rooms for her— a large, sunny room overlooking the moors, with Pew Tor rising like a fortress on the skyline.

To Jenna's relief, Mickie looked well, her small face tanned and her eyes as bright as ever. There was a tiredness in the lines of her face which Jenna hoped was just the result of travelling, and she seemed thankful to be able to go straight to bed. Jenna, making sure that she had everything she needed, promised to bring her a light supper on a tray in half an hour.

'If I can stay awake that long,' Mickie observed with a weary smile. 'I feel as if I hadn't slept for a month. How people can settle down on a plane, I don't know— I'm sure I never closed my eyes once.'

'Even if you do sleep, it's not proper rest. Now, are you sure you've got all you want? I've put soap and bath oil and talc in your bathroom, but if there's anything else...'

'You've done more than enough. It's lovely.' Mickie kissed Jenna. 'Now I'm going to go straight to bed. And do you know what I'd like more than anything else? A glass of milk and a bowl of cornflakes. I really don't think I could manage any more than that.'

Jenna laughed. 'Then that's what you shall have.' She left the older woman unpacking her small overnight case, and hurried downstairs to arrange the little meal on a pretty tray. The cornflakes were dotted with some raspberries from the freezer, quickly thawed in the microwave oven, and the milk was poured into a small crystal jug, with a matching glass. Beside them she stood a tiny vase with one pink rosebud, and a small glass of orange juice.

'Looks more like breakfast than supper,' Dair remarked as he stood watching her.

'That's probably why she wants it. With all the travelling and time-changes, her body thinks it *is* breakfast time. Anyway, it's easy to eat and digest and that's what she needs just now.' Jenna paused with the tray in her hands and looked anxiously at him. 'What's the matter with her, Dair? Has she said anything?'

'Not much. She's been advised to have some tests—we'll have to arrange tomorrow about a doctor or hospital.' He rubbed his hand across his face and Jenna realised that he had had very little sleep himself during the past twenty-four hours. Mickie's plane had been delayed on the last lap of its journey and he had had to wait for some hours at Heathrow. 'It depends whether she stays here or goes back to Suffolk. I want her to stay here, of course.' He glanced at Jenna, a question in his eyes.

'Of course,' she said steadily. 'And I'll stay too, for as long as necessary.' She bit her lip and turned away. The whole conversation was so cold, so stilted—two strangers who didn't much want to know each other better. What had happened to them? What had happened to the love she had thought they shared?

But there was no time to think of that now. Mickie was upstairs, exhausted and needing food before she slept. Mickie, who looked well superficially but had had symptoms that were alarming enough to bring her hurrying home from the other side of the world.

Until they knew just what was wrong and some kind of treatment had been started, their own problems must be set aside.

There was little time to brood over the next few days. Mickie was obviously only too glad to stay at the farm, and Dair was kept busy for the next few days arranging for her to see a doctor, who immediately referred her to the Plymouth hospital for investigation. The preliminary tests, they were told, could be carried out by the Outpatients department and, unless there were an emergency, Mickie would not be asked to go into hospital until after Christmas. But as Mickie remarked, with an apologetic glance at Dair, waiting time was so long that the only difference between being an Outpatient and an In-Patient was that she didn't have a bed.

'You really don't have to wait with me all those hours,' she said. 'You must have far too much to do. I can quite easily manage alone.'

'I've no intention of leaving you there alone, so let's hear no more about it. And there's not so much I can do about the farm at this time of year—we don't start lambing until the New Year, thank goodness.'

'I could go in with Aunt Mickie,' Jenna offered, but he shook his head.

'No—you really *are* busy. The shop's taking up all your time at present.'

That was true enough, Jenna thought. She had been surprised herself by the amount of trade they were doing—not only in Christmas wreaths but in orders for flower arrangements and bouquets to be delivered in Christmas week itself. She and Cindy had also begun a line of decorations, using dried flowers, fir cones, small logs—anything that could be combined to give a Christmassy feel when embellished with scarlet candles or sparkling frosting. An assortment of these in the window had brought customers flocking in, and Cindy's afternoons with Tanya had been spent largely in collecting the materials on their walks.

Jenna had enjoyed it all, but she had to admit that it was all very tiring. Her life seemed to be conducted at a run nowadays—even with Mrs Endicott's help, there was a lot to do at home, for she insisted on looking after Aunt Mickie herself when the older woman returned home worn out after a long wait at the hospital. And, more than that, trying to maintain the façade of a happy marriage took every ounce of strength; she had agreed with Dair that Mickie must not be worried at this stage, but when she sank into bed at night after an evening of pretence she was exhausted. It was no wonder that then, when she was alone at last, all her own problems came flooding back. No wonder she slept badly; no wonder she woke feeling heavy-eyed, dizzy and nauseated by the thought of food.

'You're looking tired out,' Cindy remarked to her in the shop. 'I reckon it's too much for you, having Dair's aunt there.'

Jenna shook her head. 'It's not that. And I couldn't refuse—Mickie's been like a mother to him. He's all she's got. Anyway, I'm fond of her too.'

'Well, don't crack up.' Cindy looked at her critically. 'You hardly eat a thing and you're losing weight. Doesn't Dair worry about you?'

Jenna smiled ruefully. 'I don't think he has time.' But she could tell from Cindy's expression that the other girl found this difficult to believe. And that was understandable too—after all, she and Dair had only been married a few months. Wouldn't most new husbands worry about their wives looking tired and losing weight?

But Dair wasn't like most husbands. He wasn't like a husband at all, these days—he was, as she had thought before, little more than a stranger now. And her heart ached at the thought of what they had lost.

As Christmas drew nearer, the weather improved. The cold spell that had brought snow earlier in the month gave way to bright, frosty days with sunshine and, waking early on the Sunday before Christmas, Jenna decided to take herself for a walk on the moor. The fresh air and exercise might dispel the permanent headache she seemed to be suffering from lately. Cindy was right—she was tired. But it was an emotional rather than a physical tiredness, she thought, an exhaustion brought on by a deep unhappiness and the need to conceal it.

How long she would be able to cope with the situation, she did not know. And she dared not think what she would do next, or where her life might go.

She set off soon after breakfast, having made sure that Mickie had all she needed and was comfortable in the sunny bedroom.

'You're sure you'll be all right? Dair's down in the office if you want anything.'

'Of course I'll be all right. I don't know why I'm staying in bed at all, on such a lovely morning—I'm just being thoroughly lazy.' The bright, birdlike eyes examined Jenna. 'You go and have a good walk, you need the fresh air. And why not take Dair with you? He oughtn't to be spending his time in that stuffy office.'

'He's busy, Aunt Mickie.'

'Busy!' The older woman snorted. 'You're both far too busy, if you ask me. You don't spend nearly enough time together.' The eyes sharpened. 'You're more like an old married couple than newly-weds.'

'It'll be better after Christmas,' Jenna said hastily, and escaped. Aunt Mickie saw far too much, and if there was one thing she and Dair were agreed on, it was that there should be no hint of any trouble between them, at least until they knew just what was likely to happen about her illness. The final diagnosis had still not been made and they dared not upset his aunt and so possibly make her condition worse.

The quiet peace of the moor ought to have brought relief to her chaotic mind. But instead, she found herself thinking yet again in the inexorable circle that brought the past few months so vividly before her—from the moment when she had first set eyes on Dair in that London office, looking so different from the smooth businessmen who surrounded him, to the moment when she had begun to pack her suitcase to leave him.

It seemed now that their relationship must have been doomed from the start. That whirlwind romance—why hadn't she realised that a man like Dair would inevitably have some kind of past, a woman or women with whom he must have been deeply involved? Why hadn't she asked him—why hadn't she asked Aunt Mickie when Lysette's name had first been mentioned, insisted on knowing the truth about that earlier engagement?

Why had Dair been so reluctant to tell her the truth? Why had he persisted in telling her that Lysette was dead, even when he must have known that Jenna knew it for the lie it was?

And where was Lysette now? The cottage was empty. She had left—but why?

Jenna had no doubt that Dair knew quite well where Lysette had gone. He must have gone to the cottage that day, when Jenna had seen her there, and they had planned it together. Lysette would leave, he would take Jenna there to 'confront' her—and she would be gone. Proving him innocent and Jenna the victim of her own imagination. Or a meaningless trick.

But why? Why should they want to do such a thing?'

And now, she supposed, they were simply waiting for Aunt Mickie's illness to be resolved before continuing with the next part of their plan—whatever it was. Although Lysette had been quite clear about that. She intended to marry Dair, and she seemed quite sure that Dair intended to marry her.

Jenna walked on, scarcely aware of the rolling moorland scenery around her. She passed through a flock of grazing sheep and a herd of wild ponies kicked up their heels as she walked by. She was startled when she suddenly found a wet nose being pushed into her hand and, looking down, found Rob's Labrador, Gypsy, bounding at her side.

'Gypsy! Hello—what are you doing here? Where's your master?'

'Right behind you,' came Rob's cheerful voice. 'Hello, Jenna. I wasn't sure whether to approach you or not— you looked so fierce, striding along there.'

'Rob.' She stopped and he caught up with her. She looked up at his smiling face, so normal, so uncompli- cated and suddenly she felt overwhelmed by her own complex problems. 'Oh—*Rob*!'

'Hey—what's this?' He put out his hands and caught her by the shoulders. 'What are all the tears for, Jen? What's wrong—is it Dair's aunt? Cindy told me she was back.'

'No—not really. Well, partly, I suppose, we *are* worried about her, but——' She shook her head and fumbled for a handkerchief. 'I'm sorry, Rob.'

'Don't be silly.' He was holding her close against him and she could feel the warmth of his body like a benison to her confused spirit. 'Look, you remember what I told you a while ago—that I'd always be around if you needed me? I meant it, you know. If you want to talk——'

'I don't know if it would do any good.' Jenna blew her nose and gave him a watery smile. 'I hardly know what it's all about myself—I don't know if I could put it into words——'

'Try.' He watched her for a moment, then added gently, 'It's Dair, isn't it? The business about him and the girl he was engaged to—Lysette, or whatever she was called.'

Jenna gave a deep sigh. She had lived with that name so long, hearing it spoken only with the utmost reluctance by Dair, that it came as a curious anticlimax to hear it spoken by Rob, just as if it were—well, as if it were any sort of name. As common and unremarkable as . . . as Joan, or Ann, or Pat.

'Lysette,' she repeated slowly. 'Yes. That's what it is, Rob.' She remembered what she had told him a few weeks before. 'You remember I saw her at the Goose Fair?'

'Yes—what happened? I never liked to ask—I thought if you wanted me to know, you'd tell me. But I wondered occasionally. It seemed so strange, when Dair said she was dead.' He glanced at her and they started to walk on, Gypsy leaping around them. 'Was it true? Was the girl you saw someone who just looked like her?'

Jenna shook her head helplessly. 'No. It was Lysette all right— I saw her again. I talked to her.' Jenna stopped and looked up at Rob with wide eyes. 'Rob, she told me -

Dair meant to divorce me and marry her—but he *still* told me she was dead! And when we went out to the cottage where she was living, she was gone. I don't understand it—and he won't explain.'

'But he must! You can't go on like that. Why, it's nothing short of cruelty!' Rob's eyes were blazing now, angrier than she had ever seen them. 'Jenna, you can't let him treat you like this.'

'I didn't intend to,' she said tonelessly. 'I was going to leave him. But then Mickie was taken ill and—well, I couldn't go, not when she was coming home ill. I had to stay—for a while, anyway.'

'How long? Until you fade away entirely?'

'No, of course not. Just until Mickie—well——'

'Until Mickie what?' he pressed her. 'Until she gets better, if she's going to? Or...until she dies? And how long is that going to be?'

'Rob, don't! You mustn't talk like that.'

'I'm sorry. But you must face the facts, Jenna.' Suddenly Rob, the boy next door, cheerful and inconsequential, seemed to have grown up. He looked at her gravely. 'You've got your own life to lead, Jenna. If this isn't right for you, if it's making you unhappy, you should get out now, before it gets even more complicated.' He looked at her a little longer. 'You're sure you're right about this? About Dair and Lysette? You see, I can't get out of my head the way he looks at you— it's no different now from when he married you. I'd swear that man loves you, Jenna.'

'No. You're wrong.' She spoke hopelessly, shaking her head. 'He's just a very good actor. Or he's the sort of man who can even believe in his own lies. He's not like you, Rob—straightforward and honest. There are all kinds of hidden corners in Dair's personality—and they

frighten me. I'm never sure what I'm going to find next.'
She gave him a rueful smile. 'I envy you and Cindy—
your problems are so simple. Once she's convinced
herself that she doesn't simply want a father for
Tanya——'

'A father for Tanya? What do you mean?'

'Why, you know that's what's holding her back—she's
afraid she's just using you, because you'd make such a
wonderful father. Deep down, of course, she knows it's
not true—she's head over heels in love with you, and all
you have to do is wait for her to realise that. But for me
and Dair——' Jenna shook her head again. 'I wish it
were that simple.'

Rob looked at her.

'Perhaps everyone's problems look simple to anyone
else, Jenna. And if you were to ask my advice——'

'I do. I'll go mad if I don't ask someone.'

'—then I'll give it you. Go straight home, find Dair
and demand that he tells you. Not just that Lysette's
dead—but just how and when she died. Forget your sen-
sitivity over this, Jenna—so what if it does hurt him?
Haven't you been hurt too? He's got to tell you the
truth—and then you'll at least have a starting-point,
you'll have some idea of where to go next. It'll release
this stalemate you've got yourselves into. And it doesn't
need to have anything to do with his aunt, either—she
needn't even know.'

Jenna stared at him. His solution sounded so beautifully, so incredibly simple. But would it work? Would
Dair really answer her questions?

'What have you got to lose?' Rob asked, and she
nodded slowly.

'Yes—you're right. Things couldn't be any worse than
they are now.' She gave him a sudden smile. 'Thanks,

Rob. I'll go and do it now.' On a sudden impulse, she
reached up and kissed him. 'You've helped sort out my
thoughts. Maybe I can do the same for you some day.'

'Don't worry,' Rob said. 'You already have.'

Jenna found a new spring in her walk as she strode back
across the soft turf towards the farm. It was curious,
because nothing had been decided, no revelations had
been made, no promises given. But she felt almost as if
they had, as if Dair had already promised to tell her the
truth. And even though she knew that the truth was likely
to be unpleasant, it would be better than this terrible
not knowing, which she had endured now ever since the
day they had been married.

The farm lay quiet in the December sunshine. There
was still a light covering of snow on the tors that rose
behind it, craggy grey masses of rock left over from some
long-ago age. An air of timelessness hung over the yard,
empty of all modern vehicles or machinery; she half
expected to see a carriage come clattering down the track,
drawn by plumed horses, or a kitchenmaid come out of
the door with an apron filled with corn to feed clucking
hens.

But there was no one. And Jenna entered the house
to find it equally quiet and every room empty.

Deflated and vaguely uneasy, she went upstairs.
Perhaps he was with Aunt Mickie. But when she peeped
round the door of the big, sunny bedroom, only Mickie
was there, tiny and more birdlike than ever in the wide
bed.

'Hello, dear. Did you enjoy your walk? It looks lovely
out—so fresh and crisp. Dair decided to go too, when
he brought me my morning coffee—I think he hoped
you might meet.'

Jenna smiled and came over to sit by the bed. 'You mean you intended us to meet, Aunt Mickie. You sent him out after me, probably quite against his will.'

'Well, perhaps.' The bright eyes gave her a direct look. 'As I think I told you, I don't believe you spend enough time together. And—well, I thought you had something to tell him, Jenna. Something important. But perhaps I'm wrong about that ...'

Jenna stared at her. There was a twinkle in Mickie's eyes that seemed entirely unfounded—as if whatever news she thought Jenna had to impart was good news. As if ...

'What on earth are you talking about?' Jenna asked slowly. 'What do you imagine I have to tell Dair?'

'Why, that you're pregnant, of course,' Mickie said with a smile. 'You are, aren't you? I'm not mistaken? I never have been yet ...'

CHAPTER TEN

'I CAN'T believe it,' Jenna said as she and Cindy opened the shop next morning. 'It never even occurred to me—yet now I come to think of it, I suppose it's possible. But I've never forgotten to take one of my pills, never.' She didn't add that it would scarcely have mattered if she had; except for that short time when Dair had come to her bed night after night and filled her heart with both ecstasy and anguish, the pills had never been necessary. But she had been afraid to stop taking them.

'What about when you had that bug? That tummy upset that went round?'

'Well, what about it?' Jenna stared at her. 'Oh, my goodness—of course! They don't work if you're sick. It's as bad as missing one altogether.' She sat down suddenly. 'Mickie must be right. And that's why——'

'Why you've been looking so washed out and why you've been losing weight,' Cindy finished. 'You've been feeling rotten every morning, haven't you?'

'Yes, I have,' Jenna admitted. 'But I thought all that—and the other things—were just due to—well, to being under strain.' She looked at her friend and said quietly, 'There's a lot you don't know, Cindy. But I'd like to tell you. I've told Rob—he's always been like a brother to me. And if you two are going to be married—well, I'd like you to know anyway.'

As briefly as she could, she told Cindy the truth about her marriage, ending with her encounter with Rob on the moors yesterday. 'So I went home intending to do just that—see Dair and insist that he told me everything. But he wasn't there—and instead, Mickie dropped this bombshell.' She gazed at Cindy again. 'Pregnant! If it's true—well, it changes everything.'

'Well, the first thing to do is find-out whether it *is* true,' Cindy said briskly. 'How reliable do you think his aunt is?'

'Oh, I'm sure she's right. She used to look after practically the whole village back in Suffolk and she says she always knew when a girl was pregnant. There's a "look", apparently—and I have it. She's been waiting for Dair and me to tell her the news and, when we didn't, she realised I hadn't even told him yet. Not surprising, when I didn't know it myself!' Jenna gave a short laugh. 'Honestly, Cindy, I must have been living in a dream— how I didn't realise, I can't begin to imagine.'

'I can. You've had a bad time, Jenna—the sort of worries that could cause just the kind of symptoms you've been having, without any possibility of pregnancy. But still, I think you ought to go and see the doctor. Why don't you make an appointment now?'

'I already have. I'm going this afternoon. Then I'll know for sure—and I'll have to make up my mind what happens next.'

'Do—do you want this baby?' Cindy asked diffidently.

'Want it? I haven't even thought in those terms, Cindy. If it does exist—and I'm sure now that it does—well, that's it, isn't it. It *exists*. It's there—my baby.'

'Yours and Dair's,' Cindy said softly.

'Yes. Mine and Dair's.'

The thought stayed with her all morning as she worked in the back room of the shop or served customers at the front. After the long talk she'd had with Cindy, she seemed to have no more words, wanted simply to retreat into her thoughts. And Cindy seemed to understand this. She worked quietly, leaving Jenna alone as much as possible. And when lunchtime came, she announced that she would stay at the shop that afternoon so that Jenna could go to the doctor and then straight home to the farm, if that was what she wanted.

'But what about Tanya? Does your mother mind looking after her?'

'Oh, Tanya's all right—she's spending the day out at the cottage with Rob. The playschool's on holiday this week,' Cindy reminded her. 'And Rob—well, he came over yesterday afternoon and suggested it.' She gave Jenna a sudden shy glance. 'This might not be the right time to tell you how happy I am,' she said, blushing. 'But—well, Rob told me he'd talked to you yesterday. And everything's all right now. We're going to be married in the spring.'

'Oh, that's marvellous!' Jenna exclaimed with real pleasure. 'And I'm sure Tanya's delighted. You'll make a lovely family, the three of you.'

Cindy smiled. 'Well, I won't say we wouldn't have got there without your help—but what you said did clear things up. And it made me see—well, that there shouldn't ever be secrets between people who love each other. We ought to be able to talk to each other, or things that don't really matter at all turn into real problems.' She blushed again and laughed a little self-consciously. 'You get yourself sorted out now,' she advised. 'Maybe you'll find your problems get solved in a way you never dreamed of.'

'Maybe,' said Jenna. But although she smiled at Cindy, she said it without conviction.

'. . . and I would say you'll have your baby somewhere around the eighteenth of July next year,' the doctor said, going back to his desk. 'So you're just over two months pregnant now. You've been having morning sickness?'

'Well, I suppose so. I' 'e been feeling a bit queasy, it's true.'

'Good. That'll soon die down and then you'll probably feel perfectly fit. But I'll arrange for you to attend some pre-natal classes, and you'll need to decide where you're going to have your baby. The hospital has a very good baby unit, or you may decide to go to a private maternity home. You'll want to discuss that with your husband, of course . . .'

He went on talking, while Jenna's mind whirled. A baby! She really was having a baby. *Dair's* baby. The doctor was talking now about a host of considerations that had never even entered her head. How long she should work . . . maternity benefits . . . natural birth, epidurals . . . The words swam into her head and out again as she sat there, too dazed to absorb them.

How could she possibly begin to think about these things, when she didn't even know if her marriage would last until next July?

As she left the surgery, her mind was filled with only one thought.

Dair. He had to know this. He had to be told. And then—perhaps—he would tell her the truth at last. He would see—surely—that it couldn't be hidden any longer.

He would have to tell her exactly what had been going on between himself and Lysette. What he intended the future to hold. What was going to happen to them all— to him and Jenna. To their child.

She remembered Cindy saying how tragic it was, how bitter she had felt, that Tanya had never known her father, saying that she would have done anything to give her child what she had missed. Believing in the right of every child to have a father so passionately that she was afraid of her own motives in marrying Rob.

Was the child that Jenna was carrying at this moment going to be born fatherless? And if she and Dair did stay together after all—would it be because they loved each other, or for the sake of the child they had conceived? Could such a marriage possibly work?

Jenna was still confused when she arrived home, but two things were clear in her mind. She could not leave Dair while Aunt Mickie was still in the house, and she had to tell him about the baby. What would happen after that, she could not begin to imagine; she could only hope.

Exactly what she was hoping for, she wasn't quite so sure.

The Range Rover, parked in the yard, told her that Dair was at home, and she went in, still rehearsing the words she would say to him. But even as she entered the big, warm kitchen, she was aware that something was wrong. And when Dair came in from the hall and she saw his face, she knew that it was something very wrong indeed.

'Dair, what is it? Aunt Mickie...?'

He nodded. His face was drawn with worry. 'She's been taken into hospital, Jenna. There was a haemorrhage... They're operating immediately.'

'Oh, no.' She sank down on a chair, her hands going immediately, protectively, to her stomach, and stared up at him.

'I've been trying to contact you,' he said distractedly, running his fingers through his hair. 'Cindy told me you'd taken the afternoon off... I've got to go to the hospital straight away, Jenna. I've only been waiting till you came home.'

'I'll come with you.' She was on her feet, her mind going immediately to the things that needed to be done before they could leave the house. 'Give me fifteen minutes, Dair.'

'You don't have to come,' he said. 'Aunt Mickie's my responsibility. You've got enough to do.'

Jenna stopped and faced him. She saw his face, grey with anxiety, his eyes lost and vulnerable, and she was conscious of a rush of love for him. Whatever had happened between them, however badly things had gone wrong, her love for him had never really faltered. That was why she had been hurt so much... but there was no time to think of that now.

'I want to come,' she said quietly. 'I love her too, you know. And—I want to be with you... if you want me to.'

He stared at her and his mouth twisted suddenly. Almost blindly, he reached out his hands and Jenna moved forward and went into his arms. They held each other close.

'Want you?' he said thickly. 'Oh, Jenna, if you only knew...'

And for a moment it was as it had always been, with all doubts swept aside, and they were as close as they had been in London, in the days before their marriage, when there had been no clouds on their horizon, no secrets, no Lysette...

Jenna stood still for a moment in the circle of his arms, then she drew gently away.

'I'll be with you in fifteen minutes,' she whispered, and slipped away.

The hospital was half an hour's drive away, in Plymouth. Dair drove as fast as was safe on the moorland road that divided Tavistock from the city, telling Jenna on the way how Aunt Mickie had suddenly been taken ill while they were both out and only Mrs Endicott had been in the house. Fortunately, she had acted quickly, calling the doctor at once, and an ambulance had been at the house within half an hour.

'If she hadn't been there, goodness only knows what might have happened,' he said tensely. 'Aunt Mickie could have died...I'd never have forgiven myself, Jenna.'

Jenna laid her hand on his thigh and pressed it gently. 'You did all you could. And she's in good hands now, Dair. I'm sure they'll save her.'

'I hope they do. I hope to God they do.' He stared through the darkness and swerved to avoid a cluster of moorland ponies who were trooping across the road, oblivious of danger. 'If Aunt Mickie dies...there's no one else, Jenna.'

She swallowed. No one? Had he finally discounted her, then, given up their marriage for lost? And what of Lysette?

'You've got me, Dair,' she whispered, but he looked at her and shook his head and her heart sank.

'Dair...' she said imploringly, and saw him look away. 'Dair...please...'

'Don't let's talk about it now, Jenna. Please.' His voice was ragged. 'Just... be with me for a while. Let's just pretend...'

Pretend what? That everything was all right between them? She shook her head, baffled, but she let her hand stay where it was, warm on his thigh. Whatever he needed now, she would do all she could to provide it. Later, when all this was over—and she shivered at the thought of what that phrase might mean—they would have time to talk. And she would tell him then about the baby.

The hospital was busy with evening visitors when they arrived and it took a little time to find out just where Aunt Mickie might be. Together, they hurried along the shining corridors, Jenna's hand clasped tightly in Dair's. At last they arrived at the ward to which they had been directed, and discovered that Mickie was being prepared for the operating theatre.

'She's quite comfortable, but a little sleepy,' the nurse told them. 'You can see her for a minute if you like.' She led them into a small side ward.

Mickie was lying in a high hospital bed, looking tinier than ever. She was swathed in a white gown, her arms lying outside the sheets. Her eyes were half closed and vague, but when she saw Dair and Jenna she smiled drowsily.

'Hello there. Come to see the patient? Silly, isn't it? I thought I was doing so well, too.'

'You are. You're doing wonderfully. And once this is over, you'll be better. We'll have you home in no time at all.' Jenna bent and touched the hand that looked so pathetically small and pale, and felt the tears come into her eyes. 'We're going to stay here until—until——'

Dair stepped forward and she felt his arm round her shoulders, warm and strong. 'You're going to be all right, Aunt Mickie. This time tomorrow, you'll be sitting up asking for a cup of tea—believe me.'

The old face creased in a faint smile. 'I hear Christmas in hospital is really quite fun.'

'You'll be home before Christmas,' Dair said quietly, and his arm tightened around Jenna as Mickie's eyes closed.

'Oh, Dair...' Jenna whispered, and turned her face to his shoulder. 'Dair.'

There was a sound behind them as the nurse slipped into the room. She moved quietly to the bed and looked down at Mickie. Then she nodded.

'They're ready for her now. If you'll just go back to the waiting-room... It'll be some time, I'm afraid.'

Dair nodded. 'We'll wait.'

They looked down at Mickie as two orderlies came in green overalls to wheel the bed away. And then Mickie's eyes opened again and she looked straight up at Jenna, and then at Dair.

'Tell...' she said vaguely, and then more strongly, as if it were important, *'Tell...'*

Jenna and Dair looked at each other. They looked back at the bed, but the old eyes had closed again. And then the bed was wheeled away and there was nothing to do but wait.

'Will she live?'

The question sounded almost brutal in the small, silent waiting-room. They were alone there, with nothing but the distant sounds of a hospital at night to distract them from their thoughts. Footsteps sounded occasionally in the corridor, voices murmured as nurses walked briskly past the door, but nobody came in to disturb them. They sat close together in a limbo while somewhere in the same building surgeons fought to save Aunt Mickie's life.

Jenna regretted asking the question as soon as the words were out, but Dair only sighed and shifted a little in the small armchair.

'We shall have to wait, Jenna. We just have to wait.' He lifted his head and looked at her. 'Did you hear what she said, just before they took her away?'

'Yes.' She'd been speaking directly to her, Jenna was sure. Telling her to tell Dair about the baby. In spite of all their care, she'd sensed that something was wrong and she wanted to make sure that he knew. 'Dair——'

'She was talking to me,' he said as if he had not heard her. 'She wanted me to tell you about—about Lysette.' Although his eyes were on her, he didn't seem to see her face. 'It was one of the first things she asked me when she came home—whether I'd told you.'

Jenna stared at him. 'And what did you say?'

'I told her the truth. That I had—and you wouldn't believe me.' He dropped his head into his hands again. 'Jenna, I've been unfair to you. I did tell you the truth— but not the whole truth. I tried to avoid it—and then, when I did try to tell you, it was too late. You'd lost trust in me. I thought if I told you then, I would lose you entirely.' His voice faded in a whisper and he took a deep breath. 'And then there was the woman you saw... I didn't understand it, Jenna. And I refused to believe the obvious answer.'

'The obvious answer? I don't understand.'

'Of course you don't. Jenna—maybe this isn't the time or the place, but we're here for several hours before we have news of Aunt Mickie. We may never have such a chance again. And she wanted me to tell you.'

'Dair, are you sure?' Jenna remembered her conviction that Mickie had been speaking to her. 'Because there's something I want to tell you too. This afternoon——'

'No.' He lifted a weary hand. 'Let me tell you first, Jenna. And please—this time, listen to me.' His tone was a simple plea. 'It's a long story and it's not easy for me to tell.'

'I'll listen,' Jenna said quietly.

There was a moment's silence. Dair seemed to be searching for words. Then he reached out for her hand and held it in both of his as he began to speak.

'First of all, I have to tell you about Lysette. She was the daughter of a man who came to live in a house near us in Suffolk. A businessman—very rich, rather bombastic, the sort who thinks he can buy the local manor and be lord of it, just like that. I didn't like him much— nobody did. But he was there, a fact of village life, and we couldn't ignore him. Nor could we ignore his daughters.'

'His daughters?'

'He had two. Lysette was one—oh, she was beautiful, I have to tell you that, with long blonde hair and green eyes, and she had the personality to go with them too. Everyone said how charming she was. Charming.' He smiled wryly. 'I'm not quite sure what that word means, you know—whether it's a compliment or otherwise. But with somebody like that, you have to give them the benefit of the doubt. Until you find something to dislike, you have to like them. Everyone liked Lysette. She was like a flower—a butterfly.'

'You forget,' Jenna said softly, 'I've seen her.'

Dair shook his head. 'No. No, Jenna, you haven't seen her. You haven't seen Lysette because she'd dead.' He tightened his hand around Jenna's fingers as she instinctively recoiled. 'Yes, Jenna, *dead*. I know she's dead—because *I killed her*.'

There was a moment of complete silence, utter stillness. The whole building seemed to hold its breath. Somewhere here, Jenna thought as she fought to control her shock, men and women were bending over Aunt Mickie's body, trying to cut out the disease that threatened her life. Was this really what Mickie had wanted Dair to to tell her? Was it really the truth at last?

'Dair...' she whispered.

But he wasn't listening. He was going on with his story and when she looked at him, Jenna saw that he was in another world—the world of the past.

'I fell in love with Lysette. And she fell in love with me. We announced our engagement. Her father was pleased enough—anything his precious daughter wanted was good enough for him. We started to arrange the wedding and then—well, then Lysette went off for a holiday abroad and, to cut a long story short, she met someone else. When she came home, she broke off our engagement.'

He told the story briefly, almost as if it didn't matter any more, but Jenna could imagine the pain he had suffered. She squeezed his hand and he smiled ruefully.

'Oh, I was hurt enough for a time. But I came to realise later that it would never have worked out for us. I said Lysette was like a butterfly, and she was. She flitted from man to man as a butterfly flits from flower to flower. She'd already been engaged twice, though I didn't find that out until afterwards. But there was no malice in her—she truly believed herself to be in love each time. She never intended to hurt anyone—and that's why what happened to her was so cruel.'

'But what was it? You said you—you——'

'Killed her. Yes. I did.' He turned towards her, but his eyes were opaque, still looking into that painful past. 'It was the night she broke off our engagement. I'd taken her out to dinner and we were driving home. There was nothing more to be said between us. She was—oh, sad that she'd hurt me, but so happy about the new love. Almost luminous. I didn't know how to bear it, Jenna. I must have given way for a moment. There was no reason for the crash, none that anyone could discover. We just…didn't go round the bend. There was a tree…' He covered his face with his hands. Stricken with horror, Jenna could do nothing but sit, clinging tightly to his hand as if by so doing she could somehow rescue him from his engulfing despair. 'They said she died instantly,' he said at last. 'And I—except for a bump on the head, I was unhurt. But that bump lost me the memory of those last few vital minutes. I've never known what made me crash that car.' He looked at her at last, and she saw the anguish that had prevented him from telling her the story before. 'I've never known whether it was deliberate or not,' he said in a low voice.

Jenna took a deep breath.

'Dair, of *course* it wasn't deliberate! You mustn't even think such a thing. You couldn't have done it deliberately—not you. You're not that sort of man. You wouldn't *allow* yourself to do it.' She gripped his hands tightly in hers and gazed into his eyes. 'Believe me, Dair. I *know*.'

He looked at her sceptically. 'How can you know, Jenna? Oh, everyone else told me the same thing, Aunt Mickie, even Lysette's father, they all assured me it could have been nothing more than a tragic accident. Nothing more!' he repeated bitterly. 'But how could they *know*? How could *anyone* know?'

'They know for the same reason that I know,' she said passionately. 'Because I know *you*. And I'd stake my life on your integrity.'

She stopped suddenly, hearing her own words. Would she? Was it really true? When she had believed for so long that he had lied to her—could she really say that and mean it?

And she knew that she could. It was Dair's integrity that had kept her with him, even though she had been confused by his reticence. If she hadn't known deep down that his word was to be trusted, she would have left him long ago.

He could never have deliberately aimed that car at the tree.

'Your life,' he said slowly. 'Lysette staked her life too, when she got into my car that night. I should never have tried to drive her home—I was too upset. It was sheer irresponsibility, Jenna—criminal irresponsibility.'

'No! A mistake, if you like—but no more than that. We all make mistakes, Dair, we all drive sometimes when perhaps we shouldn't—when we're feeling under the weather, when we've got a headache, when we're upset about something. Most of the time nothing happens. You were unlucky—tragically unlucky. But it was still no more than a mistake.' She looked at his shuttered

face and shook him by the shoulders. 'Aren't you allowed to make mistakes?' she demanded fiercely. 'Are
you so special, so much better than the rest of us, that
you can never be permitted the slightest error of
judgement? The rest of us can be forgiven—why not
you? Dair, you have to forgive *yourself*. You can't go
through life carrying a burden of guilt as if it were your
own private property. Didn't Lysette bear *any* of the
blame? She was the one who caused you to be upset.
All right, so she died for it—but the way you're going
on is killing you too. It's killing *me*.'

He stared at her. His eyes searched hers, seeking the
love that burned in her heart, the love that had never
yet been allowed its full and free expression. Then, with
a muffled groan, he caught her against him and she felt
one long, powerful shudder sweep through his body.

'Jenna,' he muttered against her hair. 'Jenna, what
would I do without you...?'

They sat silently for a long time, caught in each other's
arms, oblivious of the sounds outside the small waiting-
room. Nobody came to disturb them. At last he drew
away from her and searched her eyes again.

'Can you ever forgive me, Jenna?'

'If,' she said quietly, 'you'll forgive yourself.' And,
looking at him, knew that the process had begun and it
was time to return to his story.

'So if Lysette is dead,' she said slowly, 'who was it I
saw at the cottage? Because I did see someone, Dair,
and she was exactly like the girl in the photograph.'

'I know.' His mouth was grim now. 'I must admit,
Jenna, I didn't believe you. Or perhaps it would be more
true to say I didn't *want* to believe you. Because I wanted
all that part of my life to be over. I didn't want it in-

truding on my life with you.' He looked at her again. 'It was Lysette's sister, Jenna. Lena—her twin. They were almost identical to look at. But only to look at.'

'Her *sister*,' Jenna breathed. 'Lena. Of course . . . The flowers were for Ms L. Duran. But when I asked her if she was Lysette, she said yes. Or at least——' she tried to remember '—she didn't deny it.'

'No. She saw a golden opportunity to wreck my marriage. That's why she came, you see. You struck very near the truth once, you know, Jenna—you asked me, sarcastically, if Lysette had a double who also wanted to marry me—and then you said you wouldn't believe it! Well it was the truth. Lena was always possessive of Lysette, you see—she hated the idea that anyone might come between them. She was bitterly jealous when we got engaged. And when Lysette died, it was the end of the world for her. She was almost mad with grief and hatred. She turned on me. Said it was all my fault, and she'd see that I never found happiness now that I'd killed her sister. It wasn't a happy scene. It didn't help me to forgive myself.'

'It sounds horrible. And you think she came here to masquerade as Lysette and break up our marriage?'

'No, not quite—you see, she wouldn't have known that I hadn't told you everything. It was only when you gave that away the day you took the flowers to her—she saw her chance and took it. No, I think she simply came intending to play the *femme fatale*, the woman from the past, and drive a wedge between us. She wasn't very mature, you see—under that sophisticated exterior she's really rather foolish. It's just the kind of silly scheme she would hatch up, and if I'd only been able to talk to you before about Lysette, it wouldn't have had a chance of working. But somehow, I could never find the words. I was still filled with self-disgust—and our love was so precious, I couldn't take the risk of seeing the same disgust in your eyes if I told you. I couldn't face losing you—and when things went so terribly wrong, I knew it would be the finish if you knew the truth.'

'But why didn't you think it might be Lena?'

'Because I thought she was in America. Her father took her there soon after Lysette's death and as far as I knew she was still there, living in California. I had no idea she was back in England—and the idea that she might be playing such silly tricks simply never occurred to me. It was Aunt Mickie who told me Lena was back in England—she'd had a letter from one of her friends in Suffolk, who told her. Then I realised just what had been going on.' He looked at her with remorse in his eyes. 'I wanted to tell you,' he said, 'but I thought it was too late. Only last evening, Aunt Mickie was urging me to do it. It must have been on her mind.'

Jenna sat quietly, digesting all that she had been told. At last she looked at Dair, one more question still in her eyes.

'And the photograph? The one I saw you with on the day we were married?'

'I'd only just found it, in that extra suitcase I brought to your parents' house. I'd completely forgotten it was there. It was quite a shock when I saw Lysette's face, smiling up at me, and I won't pretend I didn't feel some grief then—grief for what might have been, yes, but grief mostly because of the waste of a life. She might have broken more hearts then mine, Jenna, but she would also have made someone very happy eventually. What you saw was my last goodbye—and nothing more.'

'Oh, Dair,' she said sadly, 'if only I had asked you then.'

There was a long silence. They sat close, slowly finding ease in each other's company, in the warmth of their bodies. Jenna wanted to tell him her own news now, but she sensed that it would be better to wait. Instead, she renewed her clasp on Dair's hand and felt the warmth of his grip returning her pressure.

'I love you very much, Jenna,' he said quietly. 'You do believe that now, don't you? And if we could possibly start again...'

'We already have. And... I'll never disbelieve you again, Dair. Never.'

'And I'll never accuse you of imagining things,' he said, and there was a smile in his voice which brought a rush of relief to Jenna's heart. She turned to look at him, and he drew her close and lifted her face with tender fingers. His eyes were clear now, swept clean of all pain, filled only with love. And her heart rose gladly to return it.

She offered him her lips and the kiss they shared was a testimony to the love that had never, through all their torment, died.

They were still sitting close, their arms wound around each other, when the door opened and the surgeon came in. He looked tired but satisfied and as Dair and Jenna came quickly to their feet, their faces filled with anxious questions, he nodded.

'Your aunt's had her operation,' he said. 'She's sleeping now, but she'll wake for a minute or two soon and if you'd like to be with her—I know it will be a great comfort to her to see you there.'

'She's all right?' Jenna breathed. 'It was a success?'

'As far as we can tell, yes.' He looked down at her with compassion. 'She's not entirely out of the wood—it'll be a little while before we can be absolutely sure. But—yes, barring complications, I think she's going to be all right. She's got a strong constitution. It all depends really on her own will to live.'

'And she has plenty of that,' Dair said. He held out his hand. 'Thank you very much. We're very grateful.'

The surgeon nodded. 'Now, if you'd like to see her...'

They followed him back to the small side ward where they had seen Mickie before. At the door, Jenna felt for Dair's hand. Together, they went in.

She was like a wraith, almost as white as the sheets that covered her, her small body barely lifting the covers as she breathed. But as Jenna sat down beside the bed, with Dair standing just behind her, the almost transparent eyelids fluttered and the bright eyes looked into hers.

'Aunt Mickie—it's me, Jenna. It's all over. You've had your operation—you're going to be all right.' She leant over the small white face. 'Did you hear that? You're going to be all right.'

Mickie's lips parted and a whisper of sound came out. Jenna leant close and heard the tiny thread of her voice. She looked up at Dair and beckoned him to bend down.

'Don't try to talk, Aunt Mickie. Just go to sleep again.'

'But I must...you must...' The frail voice faded, then returned with more strength. 'Did you tell...? Did you...?' The words trailed away and Jenna looked at her husband.

'Yes, Aunt Mickie,' Dair said gently. 'I told Jenna everything. She understands now, understands it all. It's all right—everything's all right. We just want you to get better now.'

'And I've got something to tell you both,' Jenna said, knowing that this was the moment. 'You were right, Aunt Mickie—I'm going to have a baby.' She looked up at Dair and her eyes stung with tears as she saw his face light with incredulous joy. 'You're going to be a great-aunt,' she said to the tiny figure in the bed. 'And you, my love——' she reached up and wound her arms around his neck '—are going to be a father.'

His eyes still dazed, he bent to kiss her. Behind them, the surgeon coughed discreetly. And in the bed, the old lady smiled and slipped into a gentle, healing sleep.

HARLEQUIN
Romance

A Christmas tradition...

Imagine spending Christmas in New Orleans with a blind stranger and his aged guide dog—when you're supposed to be there on your honeymoon!
#3163 Every Kind of Heaven
by Bethany Campbell

Imagine spending Christmas with a man you once "married"—in a mock ceremony at the age of eight!
#3166 The Forgetful Bride
by Debbie Macomber

Available in December 1991, wherever Harlequin books are sold.

RXM

Harlequin
HISTORICAL

CHRISTMAS
STORIES · 1991

Bring back heartwarming memories of Christmas past,
with Historical Christmas Stories 1991, a collection of
romantic stories by three popular authors:

Christmas Yet To Come
by Lynda Trent
A Season of Joy
by Caryn Cameron
Fortune's Gift
by DeLoras Scott
A perfect Christmas gift!

Don't miss these heartwarming stories, available in December at your favorite
retail outlet. Or order your copy now by sending your name, address, zip or
postal code, along with a check or money order for $4.99 (please do not send
cash), plus 75¢ postage and handling ($1.00 in Canada), payable to Harlequin
Books to:

In the U.S.

3010 Walden Ave.
P.O. Box 1396
Buffalo, NY 14269-1396

In Canada

P.O. Box 609
Fort Erie, Ontario
L2A 5X3

Please specify book title with your order.
Canadian residents add applicable federal and provincial taxes.

XM-91-2

HARLEQUIN
PROUDLY PRESENTS
A DAZZLING NEW CONCEPT IN ROMANCE FICTION

One small town—twelve terrific love stories

Welcome to Tyler, Wisconsin—a town full of people
you'll enjoy getting to know, memorable friends and
unforgettable lovers, and a long-buried secret that
lurks beneath its serene surface....

JOIN US FOR A YEAR IN THE LIFE OF TYLER

Each book set in Tyler is a self-contained love story;
together, the twelve novels stitch the fabric of a
community.

LOSE YOUR HEART TO TYLER!

The excitement begins in March 1992, with
WHIRLWIND, by Nancy Martin. When lively, brash
Liza Baron arrives home unexpectedly, she moves
into the old family lodge, where the silent and
mysterious Cliff Forrester has been living in seclusion
for years....

WATCH FOR ALL TWELVE BOOKS
OF THE TYLER SERIES
Available wherever Harlequin books are sold

HARLEQUIN
Romance®

**This December, travel to
Northport, Massachusetts,
with Harlequin Romance
FIRST CLASS title #3164,
A TOUCH OF FORGIVENESS
by Emma Goldrick**

Folks in Northport called Kitty the meanest woman in town,
but she couldn't forget how they had duped her brother and
exploited her family's land. It was hard to be mean, though,
when Joel Carmody was around—his calm, good humor
made Kitty feel like a new woman. Nevertheless, a Carmody
was a Carmody, and the name meant money and power to
the townspeople.... Could Kitty really trust Joel, or was he
like all the rest?
